## TWO DOWN

Six rounds had been fired in twenty seconds by the two men bursting into Books' bedroom. Books had counted.

Coming out from under his bed like a reptile striking from a crevice, Books fired twice at the man to his left, heard the smack of lead into flesh, then recoiled below.

The man grunted, fell backward, crashing against the washbowl to the floor.

Crouched over the bed, the other intruder fired at Books' gunflash, the bullet splintering a table.

Instantly, levering himself even with the upper edge of the mattress, Books fired once at him. The man staggered backward to the wall.

"I'm gunshot, Books!" he yelled. "Jesus Christ, don't kill me."

"You tried to kill me," Books said hoarsely. "So long, you murdering son of a bitch."

*There was a lot of life in J.B. Books yet—and a lot of death. . . .*

# THE
# SHOOTIST

## GLENDON SWARTHOUT

A SIGNET BOOK

NEW AMERICAN LIBRARY

*For*
*Tom Rosenthal*

## PUBLISHER'S NOTE

This novel is a work of fiction. Names, characters, places, and incidents either are the product of the author's imagination or are used fictitiously, and any resemblance to actual persons, living or dead, events, or locales is entirely coincidental.

NAL BOOKS ARE AVAILABLE AT QUANTITY DISCOUNTS WHEN USED TO PROMOTE PRODUCTS OR SERVICES. FOR INFORMATION PLEASE WRITE TO PREMIUM MARKETING DIVISION, NEW AMERICAN LIBRARY, 1633 BROADWAY, NEW YORK, NEW YORK 10019.

SIGNET TRADEMARK REG. U.S. PAT. OFF. AND FOREIGN COUNTRIES
REGISTERED TRADEMARK—MARCA REGISTRADA
HECHO EN CHICAGO, U.S.A.

SIGNET, SIGNET CLASSIC, MENTOR, PLUME, MERIDIAN AND NAL BOOKS are published by New American Library, 1633 Broadway, New York, New York 10019

First Signet Printing, July, 1986

1 2 3 4 5 6 7 8 9

PRINTED IN THE UNITED STATES OF AMERICA

We doctors know
a hopeless case if—listen: there's a hell
of a good universe next door: *let's go*

e e cummings

NOTE: "Gunfighter" is a word of recent coinage. A survey of Western newspapers of the late 1800s shows that a man notorious for his skill with handguns and his willingness to use them was called, variously, a "gun man," a "man-killer," an "assassin," or a "shootist."

# One

He thought: When I get there nobody will believe I could have managed a ride like this and neither by God will I.

It was noon of a bodeful day. The sun was an eye bloodshot by dust. His horse was fistulowed. Some friction between saddle and hide, of thorn or stone or knot of thread, had created an abscess on the withers, deep and festering, the cure for which he knew was to cauterize and let the air heal by staying off the animal, but he could not stop. If the horse had suffered, he had suffered more. This was the ninth day of his ride, and the last.

He wore a gray Stetson, a black Prince Albert coat, gray vest and trousers, white shirt, gray bow tie, and boots of black lizard.

Between his backside and the saddle throat was stuffed a soft pillow of crimson velvet trimmed with golden tassels. He could not have endured the journey without the pillow. He had stolen it in Creede, Colorado, from a whorehouse.

He rode below the Organs, a bleak range trending south and east, over sand flats wrinkled with dry washes. Tied on behind his saddle were a black valise and a porcelain coffeepot. The lid of the pot had clanked monotonously all morning. He stopped and, turning slowly, untied the coffeepot, turned again, and hurled it as high into the air as he was able. He meant to draw and fire and riddle it before it hit the ground, but the effort of hurling roused such pain in his groins that he could not draw. He slumped, gripping the pommel, as the pot hit the ground and tumbled down the side of a dry wash, clanking, clanking.

There were many *bosques,* or thickets, now and he detoured them. But the trail required him to pass between two, and as he did, a man jumped from the brush and leveled an antiquated cap-and-ball pistol and croaked at him to throw down his wallet. The man was thin and elderly and reminded the horseman of his grandfather, who had been driven occasionally to desperate undertakings. He had a claw hand for a left hand, cocked perpetually at the wrist, the fingers stiff and splayed. Reining up, the rider reached inside his coat. Claw Hand waggled his gun in warning. "I am not armed," the rider assured him. "You be careful of that cannon." Slipping the wallet from inside his coat, he tossed it. The old man let his eyes follow and therefore did not see the weapon which appeared in the rider's hand as suddenly as blown sand, nor did he hear the explosion because the bullet exploded in his abdomen, crazed through the vitals, was deflected by the spine, and lodged, spent, in the socket of his left hip. He dropped his gun and fell to his knees and squealed like a stuck pig.

"Gawdamighty, you've murdered me!"

"Bring me the wallet."

"I cain't! Gawdamighty!"

"Bring it, you old bastard, or I will put another one through the same hole."

The man's claw pecked at it, his good hand stopped his stomach as though it were a barrel with the bung out, and blubbering, staggering to the horseman, he handed up the wallet.

"Thanks," said the rider, putting away wallet and weapon and taking reins.

"You ain't a-going to leave me here!"

"I am." The rider considered him. "I will do you a favor, though. You have got a bellyache you are not going to get over. You can die slow or now. If you like, I will kill you."

"Kill me!"

"If I was in your fix, I would be obliged. I am a fair shot, and you are old enough, and you don't look as if life has treated you very sporting."

Claw Hand backed off and sank to his knees again and began to wail like a child. His mouth hung open in shock. Saliva dripped from his chin.

"Suit yourself," said the man on the crimson pillow, turning as he rode on. "Don't try to hold up anybody else before you die, Granddad. You are not worth a damn at it."

In another hour under the sun obscured and irritated by dust he reached a ridge which overlooked the pass, and there before him were the town and the Rio Grande and, on the far side, Ciudad Juárez and more mountains and Old Mexico. A chill wind urged him down the ridge into the pass. He had not been in El Paso for years, and they had developed it considerably since then, he'd heard, along the lines of sin and salvation. They had churches and a Republican or two and a smart of banks and a symphony orchestra and five railroads and a lumberyard and the makings of a library. So much for sin. On the side of salvation they had ninety-some saloons, just shy of one for every hundred citizens, although municipal goody-ism had moved the gambling rooms out back or upstairs. They had a "Line" on Utah Street with some of the fanciest parlor houses and flossiest girls in Christendom. Champagne went for five dollars a bottle and the girls went for drives in carriages on Sunday. In El Paso, they said, it was "day all day in the daytime and daytime all night, too."

He thought: If Hostetler is here, and he says I am O.K., and he had better after I have come three hundred miles to see him, I will be thirty years old again in thirty seconds. I will take the best room in the Grand Central or the Orndorff Hotel. I will dine on oysters and *palomitas* and wash them down with white wine. Then I will go to the Acme or Keating's or the Big Gold Bar and sit down and draw my cards and fill an inside straight and win myself a thousand dollars. Then I will go to the Red Light or the Monte Carlo and dance the floor afire. Then I will go to a parlor house and have them top up a bathtub with French champagne and I will strip and dive into it with a bare-assed blonde and a redhead and an octoroon and the four of us will get completely presoginated and laugh and let long bubbly farts at hell and baptize each other in the name of the Trick, the Prick, and the Piper-Heidsieck.

\*   \*   \*

On that prospect he clucked the roan into a trot, sharpening the anguish in his groins, and cursed himself for thinking thirty and putting the cart before the horse.

He entered El Paso sideways, from the west, avoiding Santa Fe Street and the plaza like the plague. It would not do to be recognized yet, not until Hostetler gave him the good news. He turned south on Chihuahua Street and was beset by wagons, gigs, and buckboards. He could scarcely identify the town. Most of the hospitable old adobes had been replaced by two-story buildings with brick fronts and false cornices. At intervals were tall poles strung with lines which he gradually understood to be poles and lines for telephones and electric lights. The next thing, he expected, would be herds of horseless carriages. At this rate El Paso would soon be as citified as Denver, far too highfalutin for a man who liked to let the badger loose now and then. The streets, however, were still the same chuckhole sand and gravel.

At the corner of Chihuahua and Overland a newsboy yawped. He reined up and flipped a nickel and glanced at the front page to find out what was going on in the world. It was the El Paso *Daily Herald* for Tuesday, January 22, 1901. There were two enormous headlines: QUEEN VICTORIA IS DEAD and LONG LIVE THE KING. He read the lead item:

London, Jan. 22—Queen Victoria has just died. Her last moments were free from pain. She had been in a comatose condition for some time. Her deathbed was surrounded by members of the royal family, who stood silently as the most famous monarch of the century passed into the great beyond. Preparations began at once to convey the news officially to the Prince of Wales and crown him Edward VII.

Folding the paper, he pushed it into a pocket and turned east onto Overland Street, looking left and right. Several houses had "Board and Room" signs, but one, a new two-story brick with a front porch, a wooden sidewalk, and a picket fence, displayed a smaller sign which said "Lodging." The simplicity appealed to him. It had class. He reined up and wondered if now, after nine days, he could get off the train by himself.

He eased the pillow from under him. Lifting his right leg over and down caused him such agony that after he had his left boot clear of the stirrup he had to lean for a moment, forehead resting against the cantle, sweating. He tucked the pillow under an arm then, tied the roan to the picket fence, and walked on unreliable legs up the steps and knocked at the door of the house, a double door with stained glass insert panels.

A woman opened it. He wanted board and room for a day or two. She said she preferred more permanent lodgers. He persisted, saying he had ridden nine days and was too tired to scout around. She let him in to see the room. It was at a rear corner, downstairs, through an entry after a parlor on one side, a dining room on the other. It had a south window and a west and a washbowl with running water. The bathroom, she said, was down the hall, and the rate would be two dollars a day.

"That bed is not ticky, is it?"

"It certainly is not."

"I will take my meals in here."

"I serve in the dining room."

"I will give you three dollars a day."

She hesitated. "Oh, very well. Since you're only staying a day or two."

"Can anyone around here run errands?"

"I have a son. Gillom."

"Have him take my horse to a livery. And bring in my valise first. Then look up a doctor named Hostetler and have him come see me."

"You can telephone the doctor. We have a telephone."

"I don't know how. And I do not feel up to learning today. You do it."

"You sound like a man accustomed to giving orders."

"No, ma'am. To doing as I please."

"I see."

She left him. Opening the taps at the bowl, he washed his face and hands, then placed the crimson pillow in a leather armchair, sat down gingerly, elongated his legs, and closed his eyes.

In a few minutes she brought the valise. "On the bed," he said, eyes closed.

"I called Dr. Hostetler. He'll stop by soon. He wanted to know your name."

"Who else rooms here?"

"I have three regulars. Two railroad men and a schoolteacher, a woman. They're upstairs. I am Mrs. Rogers. I don't know your name."

"Is it necessary?"

"For anyone living under my roof, it is."

He opened his eyes and considered her. She was forty, he supposed, with a decent face and a strong body and white collar and cuffs and a husband, he

supposed, who wore an eyeshade and sleeve garters and sat at a desk and made love to her once a
week, in the dark after a bath. The West was
filling up with women like her, and he would not
give a pinch of dried owl shit for the lot of them.
"Hickok," he said. "William Hickok."

"Where do you hail from, Mr. Hickok?"

"Abilene, Kansas."

"I've heard that's a wild and woolly town."

"It is."

"What do you do there?"

"I am the U.S. Marshal."

"Oh. That's nice."

"No, it isn't."

She bit her lip. "I'm glad you're not staying long,
Mr. Hickok. I don't believe I like you."

"Not many do, Mrs. Rogers," he said.

She backed toward the door.

"But I am widely respected," he assured her.


From a corner of the south window Gillom Rogers spied on the new lodger. The man unpacked
his valise and put things in a drawer of the chiffonier, then hung his Prince Albert coat in the closet.
When he turned from the closet he was in shirt
and vest. The boy's eyes rounded. Sewn to each
side of the vest was a holster, reversed, and in
each holster was a pistol, butt forward. As he
watched, sucking in his breath, the man took the
weapons out, revolved the cylinders, filled a chamber in one he had evidently fired, and replaced
them before hanging the vest, too, in the closet.
The pistols were a pair of nickel-plated, short-
barreled, unsighted, double-action .44 Remingtons,

obviously manufactured to order. The handle of one was black gutta-percha, the other of pearl.

Gillom slipped away to take the horse to the livery, letting the breath of revelation out of his lungs. He was seventeen, and spent much of his time in saloons. He was not yet served, but he enjoyed himself and picked up a great deal of miscellaneous information, some of it true, some of it of doubtful authenticity. But the man in the corner room was no stranger to him now. He had heard enough scalp-itch, blood-freeze stories to know that only one man carried a similar pair of guns in a similar manner.

He had taken a bottle of whiskey from his valise and set it on the closet shelf. Now he had a pull at the bottle and sat down on his crimson pillow and unfolded the El Paso *Daily Herald* he had bought. He skimmed the pages, waiting. He read a social item:

Mrs. Harry Carpenter gave a most delightful party Monday night at Mrs. Holm's in honor of her guest Miss Johnson. High five was the game played and after a number of games it was found that Miss Anne Martin had won the ladies' prize, a beautiful hand-painted tray. The gentlemen's prize, a lovely ebony clothes brush mounted in silver, was captured by Frank Coles. About eleven o'clock the guests were shown into the spacious dining room where delicious refreshments were served. After supper Miss Martin and Miss Trumbull delighted the audience with their beautiful singing.

He read an advertisement:

> Dr. Ng Che Hok Graduate Chinese Physician
> Over 20 years' experience in treating all dis-
> eases of men and women. He guarantees to
> cure Blood Poison, Lost Manhood, Skin Dis-
> eases, Dropsy, Hernia, Gonorrhoea, Scrofula,
> Paralysis, Rheumatism, Diseases of Brain,
> Heart, Lung, Kidneys, Liver, Bladder, and all
> Female Complaints. All diseases cured exclu-
> sively by herbs without surgical operations.
> Consultations Free.

Someone knocked at the door.

"I am Charles Hostetler."

"Doctor." He did not rise. "Have a seat." He indicated a straight chair. "Do you know me?"

"I don't think so."

"You took a bullet out of me in Bisbee, Arizona, eight years ago."

The doctor put down his bag and seated himself. "Bisbee. Let me see." He leaned forward. "Books."

"That's right."

"John Bernard Books."

"That's right."

"You've changed."

"None of us gets any younger."

"Though I must say you look better than you did that night."

"I expect so. That was quite a fracas."

"You killed two men."

"They nearly did me in. The only time I was ever hit. I took one in the belly, in a restaurant, around midnight. Damned lucky for me you were handy."

"I remember. A close thing. I don't know to this day how you pulled through."

"Are you sorry?"

"Sorry?"

"You don't approve of me."

"I'm a physician."

Books smiled. "How did I?"

"What?"

"Pull through. Tell me what you did."

"In detail?"

"In detail."

Charles Hostetler removed his spectacles and polished the lenses. "Well, as I recall, you were hemorrhaging internally. Bleeding. Entry of the bullet was on the median line of the epigastric region, and it emerged about three inches above the crest of the ilium. We laid you out on a table in the restaurant and some miners held lamps. A barber friend of mine administered anesthesia. I carbolized everything—my hands, instruments, sponges, even the table. I opened the abdominal cavity and flushed it out with two gallons of hot water, which stopped the hemorrhaging. I sutured up the liver and and repaired the gastric perforations and sewed you up again. Simple as that."

"Simple hell."

"I was sure shock would kill you, but it didn't. You must have the constitution of an ox."

"We'll see. That's why I am here."

"Oh?" The doctor put on his spectacles.

Books made a church of his fingers. "Ten days ago I was in Creede, Colorado. I hadn't been feeling up to snuff for a month or so. I went to a doc there and was examined. The next day I got on my horse and started for El Paso. I heard you were practicing here."

"What did my colleague in Creede say?"

"I won't tell you. I want you to examine me and tell me. Then I'll tell you."

"You don't trust me."

"You saved my life."

"Then you don't trust my profession."

"Doc, if I went around trusting, I'd be dead many times over."

Hostetler smiled. "All right. I'll examine you. But if I'm to know what to look for, you'll have to tell me what bothers you."

"Fair enough. I hurt. I hurt like sin. Here, in the crotch." Books pointed at the pillow under him. "I've been hurting for two months, and it gets worse. At first I thought it might be an old dose of clap, raring up on me again, but I was cured of that. Also I have trouble with my waterworks. It hurts to piddle, and I am slow as Job's goat at it."

The doctor listened. "Pain in the lumbar spine?"

"Lumbar?"

"Lower."

"Yes."

"Noticed any loss of weight?"

"I might be a bit puny."

Hostetler nodded, thinking. "All right. Take off your clothes."

Books began to do so, and while he did, the doctor removed his coat, rolled up his right shirt sleeve, washed his hands at the bowl, dried them, opened his bag, took out a jar of petroleum jelly, and lubricated his right index finger.

Books faced him, in longjohns.

"Kneel on the bed, hind end to me," Hostetler ordered. "Trapdoor down."

"You may dress now," said Hostetler.

Books dressed, and the doctor washed his hands, dried them, closed his bag, rolled down his sleeve, buttoned the cuff, donned his coat again, and seated himself. Books stood, an elbow on the chiffonier.

"Well?"

The doctor cleared his throat. "Books, every few days I have to tell a man or a woman something I don't want to. I'm not very good at it. I have practiced medicine for twenty-nine years, and I still don't know how to do it well."

"Call a spade a spade."

"How old are you?"

"Fifty-one."

"All right." Hostetler crossed his legs. "You have a carcinoma of the prostate."

"Carcinoma?"

"Cancer. That's the general term. In your case there has been considerable metastasis—spreading. When I examine you rectally I find a hard, rock-like mass spreading laterally from the prostate gland to the base of the bladder to the rectum. Is this what the man in Creede told you?"

"Yes."

"You didn't believe him?"

"No."

"Do you believe me?"

"Can't you cut it out?"

"It's too far advanced. I'd have to gut you like a fish."

"What can you do?"

"Very little. Palliation. Keep you warm and comfortable as possible. See that you eat as well as you can as long as you can. Give you drugs for the pain."

Books looked at him intently. "What you're saying is, I am a dying man."

"I am."

Books strode to the leather chair, threw the crimson pillow at a wall, and sat down, making a strange, twisted face. "I will be God damned."

"I'm sorry," said Hostetler.

"No, you're not. I said, you don't approve of me."

"That's neither here nor there. You're a human being and my patient. Therefore I'm sorry."

Books stared out a window. "I never expected to go this way."

"I'm sure you didn't."

"If I'd known this was coming."

"If it's any consolation, no one does."

"How long have I got?"

"There's no way to tell. You must be in a lot of pain already. For the life of me, I don't know how you rode down from Colorado in your condition. That, by the way, may have done you damage. Hurried matters along, I mean. Excitation of the cells."

"You said I am strong as an ox."

"Even an ox dies."

"Put it this way. If you were a betting man, how long would you say?"

"Two months. Three months. Six weeks."

"You betting wind or money?"

"Money."

"Will it be a hard death?"

"I'm afraid so."

"Can I go out? Can I have a drink? Can I play cards? Can I make love to a woman?"

"For a while. Later on you won't want to. Or be able to."

"How much later?"

The doctor shrugged. "You'll know when."

"God damn it."

"Books, I am sorry."

"So am I."

Charles Hostetler looked at the watch in his vest. "I must go. Another call to make, a pregnancy, any day now. That's the way it goes. I'll stop by tomorrow with something for you to take. For the pain. Oh, and I'll bring a book along, so you can read up on carcinoma. If you care to."

"I care to."

The doctor rose, picked up his bag.

"You can do me a favor," Books said. "Keep it to yourself I am in town."

"I surely will."

"I guess you won't mention I am a goner."

"I won't. That's your privilege." The doctor went to the door. "See you tomorrow."

There was no answer.

He sat for some time after Hostetler had gone, a man of stone. He was exhausted. The wind which had trailed him to El Paso continued to blow outside, begging round the corners of the house to be let in, and though the windows were closed, over the wind he heard, once, a high ringing sound, iron on iron, like that of clapper on bell.

He thought: Well. I am not going to the Orndorff, or the Big Gold Bar, or the Red Light, or a parlor house. So long, bare-assed blonde. Good-by, redhead. Farewell, octoroon. I am going to hole up in this room and die like some animal. In two months, three months, six weeks. And a hard death to boot. That will pleasure hell out of a lot of people. But I will not think about it now. I will have a drink and read the paper.

He stood up, took the whiskey bottle from the closet shelf and had a long pull, replaced his pillow in the armchair seat, picked up his paper, and sat down again.

He thought: This is the last newspaper I will ever read. I won't buy another. I have skimmed newspapers all my life and never got the whole good out of one. Well, I will read every word in this one and when done I will know for a fact what was going on in the world on the twenty-second day of January in the year 1901. It is a damned important day to me. For a sizable part of it, I did not know I was about to die, so in a way it was my last one alive. From now on, however many days I am allowed, they will all be downhill.

The first item which caught his attention was on the front page:

Cowes, Isle of Wight, Jan. 22—The death mask of the queen will be made by Mr. Theed, the famous sculptor. He was summoned to Osborne House on Sunday to be in readiness for the work. Artists and sculptors the world over are interested in Mr. Theed's important mission.

He thought: I will not break. I won't tell anybody what a tight I am in. I will keep my pride. And my guns loaded to the last.

# Two

Gillom Rogers slept late, then yawned downstairs to the dining room. The regulars, the two railroaders and the teacher, had long ago breakfasted and gone, and the house was quiet. His mother sat opposite while he ate, sipping coffee and appraising her son as though to sustain a conviction that he could not yet be a man. Shave or not, tall or not, handsome or not, profane or not, intractable or not, seventeen, she believed, was still a boy.

Gillom nodded toward the rear room. "He in there?"

"Yes."

"What'd you feed him? Horseshoe nails and a cup of coal oil?"

"Sshh. He'll hear you."

"Who gives a damn."

She recalled washing out his mouth with soap when he was ten. "School this afternoon?"

"Hah."

"What, then?"

He tilted his chair to reflect. "Let's see. The Connie first, I guess."

"They won't serve you."

"I'll get roaring drunk, then go on down the Line and raise hell till they throw me in the *juzgado*."

"Gillom."

"Well? Mind your own business."

In the entry, a clock ticked.

"Don't speak to me that way," she said. "If your father were here, he'd—"

Gillom banged his chair down and braced his hands against the table as though to tip it over. "I've told you, Ma," he warned. "Don't talk to me about him. Don't ever, I won't have it."

"I am not to use his name in your presence."

"That's what I said."

It was a boyish call to battle she must accept. If she stood her ground, told him the truth, she might gain an enemy, but if she permitted him to bully her into retreat, she lost more than a skirmish: she lost a son. So she mustered herself. She met his scowl with a composure seventeen could never match.

"I love you," she said. "You know that, and take advantage of it. But the truth is, I loved him more. I always did, I always will."

He let go of the table, then did not know what to do with his hands.

"If it grieves you, I will never mention your father again. But I will speak of my husband whenever I wish."

She won, temporarily at least, and at what cost she could not estimate. He saucered his coffee, blew to cool, then attacked again, as the young do, this time from the flank.

"School. It don't amount to a hill of beans. I can learn more around town."

"I hope so."

"I know so. Who do you think moved in with us yesterday?"

"His name is Hickok. William Hickok."

"Hah."

"He's the U. S. Marshal in Abilene, Kansas. He told me."

Gillom drank a noisy triumph. "Are you dumb, Ma. Wild Bill Hickok was shot dead in Deadwood twenty-five years ago."

"I don't believe you."

"In the back. He was playing poker. The cards he held—they call it the 'Dead Man's Hand.' A pair of—"

"Gillom."

"I saw his guns, when he got off his horse yesterday. A pair of nickel-plated Remingtons. He carries 'em in holsters sewed to his vest."

"Who?"

He could not saucer his excitement. "Ma, we've got the most famous gun man in the world nowadays! Living with us, right here on Overland Street! Oh, he's mean. He's killed thirty men!"

"Gillom, you tell me!"

"Hold your hat. J. B. Books!"

Bond Rogers' cheeks flamed. She rose, turned, steadied herself with the chair back. She stared at her son, then swept from the room.

"Come in."

She entered, but couldn't decide whether or not to close the door behind her. If she left it ajar, Gillom might overhear. If she shut it, she put herself at the mercy of a violent man, perhaps depraved. She left it open but set her back to it and clutched the knob.

"Mr. Books."

"Mrs. Rogers."

"You are J. B. Books."

"Yes, ma'am."

"You have rented my room under false pretenses."

"Sometimes I advertise, sometimes I don't."

"I will not have anyone of your stamp under my roof. I demand that you pack up and leave."

"I'm sorry."

"This is my room, I remind you. I want you out of it within the hour."

"I am sorry. I can't."

"Why not?"

"I don't propose to say."

"You will not go!"

"No."

"That is your last word."

He considered her, a rag of amusement at the corners of his mouth. "You have a fine color, ma'am," he said, "when you are on the scrap."

Confused, angered by the compliment, Bond Rogers whirled, stumbled against the door, and slammed it shut after her, only to confront her son. He stood in the hall, eavesdropping as she had suspected, but his expression stunned her. He regarded her with the same acuity, the same deliberation, the same glimmer of amusement she had just fled from, and the discovery that she might be mistaken, that he might be a man after all, not a boy, that she might in fact be alone with two strangers, both of whom had gained admission to her house under false pretenses, terrified her. Gillom did not move. She fled from him to the telephone on the wall, lifted the receiver from the hook, spun the crank, and adjusted the mouthpiece to her height.

"Central? Will you please connect me with the City Marshall's office? I don't know the number, I haven't time to look it up. Marshal Thibido. Thank you."

Moses Tarrant, who owned a livery stable on Oregon Street, stopped in the Acme Saloon. The place was almost deserted, since the gambling rooms were upstairs. A penurious man, Tarrant drank little and when he did, held it well, but on this day he could no longer hold the news he had to tell. During the osmosis of a nickel beer he informed the barkeep that J. B. Books was in El Paso. He knew Books was, he said, because he had the man-killer's horse in his stable. To Tarrant's surprise, the barkeep heard him with indifference, continuing to polish glasses with his apron and to rack them. Disgruntled, the liveryman drained his glass and departed. The instant he had gone, however, the barkeep left his bar unattended, climbed the stairs with unusual celerity, and announced to a table of five men playing draw that J. B. Books was in town. Among the players was a man named Shoup and one named Norton.

"I'm the City Marshal. Walter Thibido."

"How do you do."

"I'm told you are John Bernard Books."

"You are told right."

"I've seen your face in the papers, but I wouldn't recognize you. Must of been a young picture."

"I'm handsomer now."

The marshal was not of a mind to banter. He appeared to have dressed in his best bib and tucker for what was to him a momentous, possibly a historical, occasion—in a serge suit and a clean shirt and a brass badge and, on his right hip, in a new holster, the Peacemaker he carried only on Sundays.

"Have a seat," Books offered.

"Don't think I will."

Books noted that he held his hat in his left hand and kept his right free, his collar crimped him, his shoes squeaked, and most important, that he was breathing hard with responsibility. This signified he had nerved himself to make the supreme civic sacrifice if necessary, which made him unpredictable, which made him dangerous.

"Breathe easy, Marshal. You are closer to your gun than I am to mine. Besides, I seldom kill anybody before noon. How did you know I was here?"

"Mrs. Rogers' boy spotted you, and told her. She telephoned me."

"So you welcome me to El Paso."

Thibido was more interested in mortality than irony. "I sure as hell do not. She claims you told her you were Wild Bill Hickok or she'd never of rented you a room. She wants you out of it. I don't blame her."

"Neither do I."

"So do I want you out, Books. I checked my bulletins before I came over, and didn't find anything I could hold you for. I wish I had of. But I want you out of town. We've got five railroads here and they'll be glad to sell you a ticket to any damn where."

"I won't be hurrahed."

"I'm not trying to. I'll buy the ticket."

"For purely personal reasons."

"Purely personal."

"Such as?"

"Such as I've been marshal a year now and I like it. I sleep at home and my wife is a good cook. I've got six deputies in uniform and we draw city pay at the end of every month. I don't have to depend on fines. Such as about all we have to handle is drunks and cardsharks and a robbery and a knifing now and then and what I don't need is a genuine rough customer like you. You dally here and you'll draw trouble like an outhouse draws flies. So I want you on your way far away. Directly. Today."

"I might not be inclined."

"Then I will by God incline you. I told you, I have six deputies and I can badge as many men as I need. We will smoke you out or carry you out feet first, and the Council will back me up. So you say which, Mr. Gun Man. It's your funeral."

Books considered him. By the end of his peroration he was red in the face and breathing harder and shifting from foot to foot on his squeaky shoes. He was also flexing and unflexing the fingers of his right hand and saying inside, probably, a prayer.

"I can't go," said Books.

"Can't?"

"No. I am in a tight."

"You'll be in a worse."

"Not worse than this. I have a cancer."

"A cancer?"

"Of the prostate."

"That's too thin."

"Ask the doc, Hostetler. That's why I came down

here from Colorado, to see him. He examined me yesterday. I don't have long. I will die in this room."

Walter Thibido was a small muscular man in his forties. He looked at Books and his face worked. Suddenly he dropped into a chair, bent forward, elbows on knees, face in hands, and through his fingers expelled relief.

"Whoo. Whooeee."

He reminded Books of someone who had just stepped from a Turkish bath into a cold shower.

"I tell you the truth, Books. When I came here I was scared," he said, smiling through his fingers. "I know what a man like you is capable of when he's cornered. On the way I wondered who'd get my job, and if the Council would give my wife a pension, and if it'd snow the day they put me under. Whooeee."

He shook his head, straightened up, found his hat. "Cancer. Cancer," he chortled. "Oh, that's rich. By God that's rich. When I think of the close calls you must of had, and now this. The great killer doesn't die of lead poisoning or a rope necktie after all—he's done in by his crotch!"

He realized what he was saying. "Excuse me if I don't pull a long face. I can't."

Books was silent. And perceptibly, as he went unchallenged, the marshal was restored to full fettle. He had done his duty and survived. He had not had to draw his weapon. He had been handed his dignity and authority on a silver platter. To the best of his knowledge, his conscience and prostate were in excellent shape. He leaned back, hooked his thumbs in his vest.

"I'm a lucky man, Books. We had bloody hell in El Paso a few years back. Wes Hardin was killed over on San Antonio Street six years ago. John Selman blew his brains out. Then George Scarborough killed Selman. Then some tough—Will Carver maybe—killed Scarborough. Before that, Dallas Stoudenmire killed Hale and Frank Manning killed him. Oh, we've had more than our share. Well, when they hired me last year I thought, This is a new century, the hard cases have killed each other off, the wheel of fortune has finally stopped, I can be a peace officer and stay healthy and someday die in bed. Then Mrs. Rogers on the telephone. I thought, My God, I was wrong, here she goes again. There is just one killer left and by God if he doesn't decide to dance one more fandango and in my town. I will have to face him. Today your string plays out, Thibido. J. B. Books is going to put out your light today. But you're not, are you?" He smiled jovially. "Cancer. If that isn't rich."

"You talk too much," Books said.

It was as good as a slap. Walter Thibido recoiled, then grimmed up and regained his earlier truculence. "As much as I damn please." He stood. "I will ask Hostetler. But I believe you. You stay put right here, where I can keep an eye on you."

"Where would I go?"

"That's right, where would you? Say, by the way, how long does he give you?"

"He doesn't know. Maybe six weeks."

"Six weeks."

"You can do me a favor, Thibido."

"I owe you one. Or Hostetler."

"Keep it under your hat I'm cashing in."

"Why?"

"My being in El Paso, maybe that's news. Dying is my own business."

"All right. Anyway, I don't want some tinhorn trying to cut your time short. Or making a liar out of Hostetler. And you can do me one."

"One."

"Let me see your guns."

"In the closet. On my vest."

A bantam rooster again, Thibido squeaked to the closet, pulled the curtain aside, felt for the vest on its hanger, and one at a time, with a kind of reverence, brought out the Remingtons. "Jesus." He inspected them professionally. "Just like I heard. Made to order."

"They were."

"Double-action?"

"Faster."

"But less accurate."

"Not if you know how."

"Modified, I suppose."

"A special mainspring, tempered. I had the factory file down the bents on the hammer, too. You get an easier letoff when you put pressure on the trigger."

"Five-and-a-half-inch barrels."

"Greased lightning."

"I'll stick to a Colt's."

"You do that."

The marshal cocked his head. "I could take them, you know. Now."

"But you wouldn't."

"Wouldn't I?"

"No." Books spoke evenly. "Because if you did, I'd go out and buy a gun, any gun. I can still get around. Then I'd come for you. Your deputies would swim the river. You'd be alone. You and I know how it would turn out. It would snow the day they buried you. So put my guns away."

It was the maximum Walter Thibido would take. He turned to the closet, and when he had pulled the curtain he fixed his hat on his head, spread his legs, and spoke as evenly as Books had.

"I also heard you are as mean a son of a bitch as ever lived. Well, you be a son of a bitch while you can. I told you, when I walked in here I was scared. No more. I'm not the one going away. You are. So be a gent and convenience everybody and do it soon. Six weeks is too long. I'll see you aren't lonesome. I'll drop in to cheer you up and watch your progress. And I'll do you another good turn."

Books waited.

"The day they lay you away, I will shit on your grave for flowers."

Books adjusted his crimson pillow. "That is a damned handsome suit you're wearing, Marshal."

A line of burros humped high with firewood for sale passed the house, coerced into a trot by a Mexican with a long cactus switch. Walter Thibido and Bond Rogers stood on her front porch.

"He is J. B. Books, isn't he?"

"Yes, ma'am, he is."

"I wouldn't have let him in the door had I known."

"I wouldn't have let him over the city limits."

"Surely he's going now."

Thibido hemmed and hawed. "Mrs. Rogers, I want to talk to you about that."

"You didn't back down!"

"I surely did not. But I'll put it to you confidentially, Mrs. Rogers. He won't be here long."

"Marshal, when my roomers find out who he is,

they'll leave like scat. I can't afford that. They are my livelihood. Do you mean to tell me I can't decide who lives on my premises and who doesn't?"

"Ma'am, he's—" He clamped his jaw. "He won't be here long."

"He certainly won't!"

She was diverted. The ice wagon stopped, and she ordered fifty pounds. She watched closely as the iceman cut the block, weighed it, wiped off the sawdust, tonged the block onto his shoulder, then directed him to take it around and in the back way and mark her card, which was tacked by the door. Thibido meanwhile pondered how to soft-soap her and looked her over and concluded he wouldn't kick if he were required to snug up to her some cold night and hoped Ray Rogers had appreciated what he had at home.

"You represent the law," she began again.

"That's what I'm getting at, Mrs. Rogers. From a police standpoint, it's safer to have him here, where I can keep an eye on him, than letting him run loose. He's a dangerous man. He won't harm you, he's not that kind—guns and gunplay are his bread and butter. If he goes to leave, you telephone me right away."

"But my roomers. When they learn—"

"Don't tell 'em. We'll keep it amongst the three of us. That's counting your boy."

"I couldn't sleep. Just the thought of such a man, sitting there hour after hour—"

"In the meantime, the city will be much obliged to you."

"Gillom says he's killed thirty men."

Walter Thibido had other matters to attend. He

struck an official pose. "Mrs. Rogers, I give you my word. He won't be with us long."

Denver, Colo., Jan. 22—This morning Claude Hilder, aged nineteen, shot Emma Douglas and Harry R. Haley, and then killed himself. The woman will probably recover. Haley is dangerously wounded in the lungs. Jealousy caused the tragedy. Hilder's brother, a returned Philippines soldier, killed himself recently, his mother also dying as the result of self-inflicted wounds. The family is said to be tainted with insanity.

Books put down the El Paso *Daily Herald*. He thought: This is where I am. A room in a rooming house on Overland Street in El Paso, Texas. I will be here until March, maybe, or April. It is the last place I will be. I had better have a close look at it.

The room was commodious, perhaps eighteen by twenty-two. The floor was wood, oak possibly, which would be dear in these parts, and the Wilton carpet was patterned with red and purple roses. Beside the bed and before the washbowl hooked oval rugs of orange and black had been laid to protect the carpet. The furnishings were quality, too: the leather armchair in which he sat; a library table between it and the bed, which was brass; under the bed a china slop-jar, along its rim a row of cherubs playing harps and providing musical accompaniment while you pissed; a straight chair; and the massive chiffonier, with five drawers. On the table, on a large doily, stood a lamp with two bulbs and pull-chains and an ornate shade. The material resembled isinglass, but it was frosted, and under this crystal coating blue, brown, and green birds of paradise were painted, so that when the lights were on the effect was vivid, almost magical. The birds seemed to take wing. On the table, under the shade, sat a glass candy compote, its cover in the shape of a stem of grapes. The compote was empty. He valued the washbowl, mirror, and towel rack. Shaving might be difficult later on, but at least he would not have to leave the room to manage it. The wallpaper featured sprays of blue and golden lilies against a white background, and there were two pictures, framed and under glass. In one, the smaller, a noble Indian sat astride his pony on a rocky promontory, surveying a wilderness with sorrowful mien. In the other, the setting was a woodland glade, and a tranquil pool about which, gazing at their reflections in the pool, knelt several nymphs, clad just diaphanously enough to reveal their rather buxom charms. They were not alone. Spying upon them from the foliage was a gang of half-men, half-goats, with horns and hoofs and hairy tails and legs, who appeared to him to be working up a lust to leap and lay hell out of the nymphs. The ceiling fixture was two bulbs suspended in glass domes. The closet curtain, on a rod, was green muslin. There were two windows with lace curtains, and the one to the south being raised, the lace was stirred by a breeze. He saw a shadow on the wall.

He eased himself off his pillow, edged along and around the bed and down the other side to the wall.

He hunched and, bending his left arm, thrust it swiftly through the open window and along the wall of the house like a hook. When his fingers met something, he seized it. He pulled.

Gillom was hauled along the wall by a suspender until his face was less than six inches from J. B. Books's face. Then another hand reached through the window and took him around the throat.

"You little bastard! You spy on me again and I'll nail your slats to a tree!"

The man had his throat in both hands now. "Recognized me, huh? Told your ma, didn't you? Who else did you blab to?"

"Mose," Gillom choked.

"Speak up!"

"Tarrant. At the stable."

He was lifted off his feet, shaken the way a terrier shakes a rat. "God damn you, boy! If you were mine I'd whip your setter so raw you'd stand the rest of your miserable life!"

Gillom did not resist. And as suddenly as he had been seized, he was let go. Books's face seemed to deform into ridges and furrows. He groaned. He went down on his knees inside the room, heavily. He turned his head sideways and rested, cheek down, on the windowsill.

Gillom withdrew a step and waited, rubbing his throat. Presently he asked, "Are you O.K., Mister Books?"

"O.K."

"Are you ailing?"

"Not as well as I might be."

Gillom chewed a lip. It was an unpleasant habit, chewing a lip and looking sour, as though he were eating himself and disliked the taste.

"Can you draw as fast, though?"

That brought up Books's head. He was prepared to let the boy have it again, both barrels, but the look on the face so near his was one of such unabashed awe, such flop-ear, wagtail admiration, that his anger was cooled, his pain assuaged.

"How did you know me, son?"

"Your guns."

"I had my coat on."

"I watched you. Through the window."

"I can't abide a skulker. If you want to see me, knock on my door like a man."

"Yes, sir."

"What about my guns?"

"Everybody's heard of 'em. Gosh. And you. You're the most famous person ever came to El Paso."

"It doesn't please your ma."

"She don't understand. Hell, she don't have the least idea who we've got living with us."

"But you do. And you can't keep your mouth shut. If you don't henceforth, I will come down hard on you."

"I will."

"Why aren't you in school?"

"Well, I quit."

"I can't tolerate a quitter, either. When you start something, finish it. Or don't start."

The boy was silent. Books grunted, got slowly off his knees. "Whatever you do, don't lollygag. Go do something useful."

Gillom grinned. "What do you do useful?"

Books was silent now. Divided by brick, they could not see each other.

"Can I fetch you anything, Mr. Books?"

"No."

"Can I shine your boots?"

"No."

"I must clean the room."

"Go ahead."

Aproned, her hair done up in a kerchief, Bond Rogers entered, carrying as subterfuge a dustcloth, a cake of Bon Ami, and a carpet sweeper. The room needed less than a lick and a promise, but she had schemed to have housework an excuse for him and a distraction for herself. She simply couldn't walk in and stand, back to the door again, or sit opposite him and have it out, she hadn't the courage. But by moving about, by keeping busy, half her mind on what she was doing, half on what she was saying, she might not only survive the ordeal, she might achieve what she wanted. She planned first to dust, and while doing so to remind him of the lie he had used to cheat his way into her house, and then, as he writhed with guilt, and as she ran the carpet sweeper, she could persuade him to betake himself elsewhere, perhaps to a den of iniquity more suitable to his appetites.

It went wrong from the start. In order to evade his eyes, to put the menace of the man in the armchair behind her, rather than dusting she began to scrub the washbowl. But that placed her next to the closet, in which hung his vest, and the proximity to his firearms gave her the shudders. She knew, too, that he was considering her, and probably her backside. She held the cake of Bon Ami to her nostrils as though it were smelling salts, but what she sniffed was vice, gunpowder, foul language, and the stench of death. And just as she opened her mouth to indict him again for taking criminal advantage of an alias, he spoke:

"I apologize, Mrs. Rogers."

"Apologize."

"For taking Hickok's name in vain."

"You should. But I will not accept it. The only way you can show repentance is to leave."

She scrubbed righteously, waiting.

"What is the sound I hear every half hour or so? Down by the corner. Like wheel rims on a wagon."

"Oh. Probably the streetcar. It passes our corner every half hour."

"The streetcar?"

"Yes. Mule-drawn. We've had them in El Paso for some time. They cross the river, too, and run back and forth from Ciudad Juárez. Mr. Books, I was asking you to leave."

"When will I have the honor of meeting Mr. Rogers?"

"My husband passed away last year."

"I am sorry."

She rinsed the bowl. "When my other roomers hear who you are, they will go, I can't stop them. This house is all I have—the income from it—and there's a loan against it at the bank. If I lose that income—"

"What did he do?"

"He was passenger agent here for the G & H, the railroad." She picked up the slippery cake of cleanser, dropped it, picked it up again, turned, and the gall of him, seated on a velvet pillow like a potentate on a throne while she did his menial chores, engendered in her the gumption she had needed from the beginning. "Mr. Books, I know all about you." She put hands on hips. "You are a vicious, notorious individual utterly lacking in character or decency."

"Passenger agent. Did he wear sleeve garters?"

"You are an assassin."

"I have been called many things."

"I believe my son. And Marshal Thibido. You've killed I don't know how many men."

"That is true."

"So you are an assassin."

"Depends which end of the gun you're on."

"Rubbish!"

He smiled. "They were in the process of trying to kill me."

The smile, the mordant tone, most of all the remark, the common sense of which was unassailable, brought color to her cheeks again in spite of herself. Distraught, she snatched the dustcloth from her apron band and commenced to do the top of the chiffonier. "You misrepresented yourself to me basely, Mr. Books. You took advantage of a widow, a helpless woman."

"I don't know about helpless. You appear to me full of vim and vinegar."

"He said you won't be here long."

"Who?"

"Mr. Thibido."

"What else did he say?"

"That you are a dangerous man—which I scarcely needed telling." She ceased to dust. She bunched the cloth as though to make a weapon of it. "Long or not, I ask you for the last time to leave my house. If you cannot be a gentleman, you can at least take pity on my situation. Sir, I demand that you go. If it will give you pleasure, I will fall on my knees and beg—"

"No."

"Damn you."

"Mrs. Rogers, I can't."

"Can't!"

"I have nowhere to go."

"There are plenty of—"

"I have a cancer."

"You—"

"I am dying of it."

"Oh."

She did not really comprehend. She tucked the cloth into her apron.

"That's why I am in El Paso, to see Doc Hostetler. He took a bullet out of me once. He was here, as you know, and examined me. I have no chance."

She moved past him to the bowl, retrieved the cake of Bon Ami. She was like a woman walking in her sleep.

"Thibido was right. I won't stay long. Two months, maybe. Six weeks."

She crossed the room again, to the carpet sweeper, took it by the handle.

"I'm sorry, ma'am. I am the one helpless. I would leave, but no one would take me in."

Bond Rogers gave way then. She sank to the far side of the bed, covered her face with her hands, burst into tears.

"I know what is troubling you," he said. "Tending me. Well, you won't have to. Just bring me my meals and I will do what else is needed. I guarantee not to be a burden."

She tried to speak but could not.

"I will make it worth your while. I will give you four dollars a day."

She said something unintelligible.

"All I ask is that you keep this between us. It's out that I am in town, I can't help that, the harm's done. But I do not want my condition known. Somebody might get the idea I can't defend myself, and I am in deep enough as it is."

"No, not in my house!" She was sobbing uncontrollably. "Oh, no, please, God, no!"

Shoup and Norton were second cousins and drunk. They were playing billiards in the Acme. Concluding the game, they refilled at the bar and took a table in a corner of the saloon, bringing with them a platter of hard-boiled eggs and flies from the free lunch.

"Bring back them eggs," said the barkeep.

"They're free, ain't they?" demanded Norton.

"You get one egg, not the bunch. Take one apiece and bring 'em back."

Shoup pulled his pistol, laid it on the table. "You talk tough t'me, you slatty sonabitch, I'll part your hair on the other side."

The barkeep was a man named Murray, called "Mount" because, though he was very thin, he was six feet, four inches tall. Stooping, he brought forth a double-barreled Parker shotgun and placed it on the bar. "See this, Shoup? I am very sure with it. You go to put finger to trigger in here and I will fire one barrel and then the other and take off your stones one at a time. Separate. Now bring back them eggs."

Shoup kept one for himself, Norton kept one, Shoup returned the platter to the bar, then sat down again. They put heads together.

"Books," said Shoup.

"Books," said Norton.

"Three blocks from here."

"Three blocks."

"Shut up. I owe 'im from way back, in San Saba County. I owe Books an' you owe me."

"Uhh-unh."

"There might could be a way. Two of us, we might could do it."

"I ain't goin' up agin' him nohow," Norton stated, lifting his egg and opening his mouth. "He's too sudden of a man."

Using the barrel of his pistol as though it were his hand, Shoup slapped egg, fingers, and mouth with one blow. Norton's eyes bulged at the impact. He choked on bloody egg. "You craven bastid," Shoup said. "I owe Books an' you owe me."


His landlady knocked and explained that a reporter from the newspaper was waiting on the porch. He wanted an interview.

"An interview? What about?"

"He didn't say."

"Send him in."

Before his visitor appeared, Books rose with some effort, straightened his tie, dropped the crimson pillow behind his chair, thought of putting on his coat, thought better of it, stood waiting.

"Mr. Books, J. B. Books, I'm most pleased to meet you, sir, and honored. The name is Dan Dobkins. I'm with the *Daily Herald*."

They shook hands. They sat down.

"As I said, Mr. Books, this is a great and unexpected honor. Thank you for seeing me, thank you very much."

"How'd you know I was in El Paso, Mr. Dobkins?"

"Why, it's common knowledge, sir. News like

that spreads like wildfire, believe me. We ran the story this morning, that you're here and stopping with Mrs. Rogers and enjoying our salubrious winter climate, so on and so forth. Have you seen it?"

"No."

"Well, it was page one, I assure you."

"What can I do for you?"

"Well, sir."

Dobkins was a spindle-shanked young fellow in his late twenties, with a long nose and yellow shoes and a striped suit and an Adam's apple which was perpetually agitated. He smelled almost romantically of toilet water and talcum powder.

"That's what I came to talk to you about, Mr. Books. You must appreciate, sir, that you are the most celebrated shootist extant."

"Extant?"

"Still existing. Alive."

"I see."

"All the others are gone, I'm sorry to say—Hickok, Masterson, the Earps, Bill Tilghman, Ringo, Hardin, Doc Holliday, Sam Bass, Rowdy Joe Lowe—all the great names."

"That's true."

"The end of an era, the sunset, you might say. You're the sole survivor, Mr. Books, and we're thankful for that—I mean, your reputation is nationwide. This morning's story went out over the wires, and every daily of any consequence will run it. But it's only a teaser. They'll want more. Papers in the East in particular—a colorful figure like you is a hero to the dudes back there. New York, Boston, Philadelphia, Washington—they'll run every word we send. Between us, Mr. Books, we can really put El Paso on the map."

"You're going the long way round the barn, Mr. Dobkins."

"Yes, sir. Well, sir, I would like tremendously to do a series of stories on John Bernard Books, the last shootist."

"A series?"

"Yes. How long will you be with us?"

"Not long."

"Oh. Well, I have a list of questions here." The reporter pulled a small note pad from his pocket. "I've made them up in advance—we could start today, right now, and get together again tomorrow."

"What kind of questions?"

"Let me see." Dobkins opened the note pad, took out a pencil. "There's been so much cheap fiction about gun men, as you know, Mr. Books. Dime novels, myths, downright lies, so on and so forth. I thought I'd get down to brass tacks for once—you know, the true story, the facts—while you're available, before anything happens to you. I mean, I hope nothing does, but—"

"The questions."

"Oh yes. Well, for example, we'd start at the beginning—your young years. What turned you to violence in the first place."

"Go on."

"These aren't questions so much as subjects. Then I'd want to cover your career factually—the statistics, you might say. How many duels you've had. How many victims."

Books nodded.

"I'd like to delve rather deeply into the psychology of the shootist—no one's ever done that seriously. How important is the instinct of self-preservation? What is the true temperament of the man-killer?

Is he the loner they say? Is he really coolheaded under fire? Is he by nature bloodthirsty? Does he brood after the deed is done? Reproach himself? Or has he lived so long with death for a companion that he is used to it—the death of others, the prospect of his own?"

Dobkins was extemporizing. Carried away by rhetoric, he seemed unaware that his host had risen and moved to the closet. Books pushed aside the curtain and reached with one arm.

"Finally, I'd like to take one of your duels as an example and dissect it step by step, shot by shot. And afterward, how did you feel inwardly, when you came through unscathed? What were your emotions as you looked down upon your foe, mortally wounded, eyes glazing, breathing his last? What were his dying words? What did you reply? Oh, I see this as a splendid climax—we'll have the reader glued to—"

Dan Dobkins swallowed the rest of his sentence. His eyes glazed. He stared into the muzzle of a gleaming pistol.

"Open your mouth," Books said.

He opened his mouth. The barrel of the Remington was introduced to his tongue by an inch or two.

"Close your mouth. Don't bite down. Make believe it's a nipple. Suck."

Dobkins did as ordered.

"Now," Books said quietly. "Notice, I have slipped the safety. This gun has a hair trigger. One fit or fidget and Mrs. Rogers will scrub your brains off the wallpaper with soap and water. Now put your pad and pencil away. Careful."

The reporter was careful.

"On your feet and start backward, toward the door. Don't shake or shiver or breathe—just suck. All right, move."

Dan Dobkins moved in slow motion, trembling, to his feet and commencing a kind of glide backward. He closed his eyes. His Adam's apple convulsed. He moaned.

"I'll open the door. You keep going. Through the entry. Easy."

Barrel in mouth, eyes closed, moaning, the reporter backed through the door and along the entry, Books following step by step. As they passed the parlor, Mrs. Rogers flew to her feet from the sofa. "Mr. Dobkins—Mr. Books, how dare you! What in heaven's name—"

"Be still, ma'am," Books warned. "We're in a touchy situation here."

She froze, hands stopping her mouth.

They reached the front doors. Reaching for the knobs, Books opened both doors and with his left hand spread them wide. He straightened, slipped the barrel of the Remington slowly from the reporter's mouth. Dobkins opened his eyes.

"Turn around."

"Please, Mr. Books, I beg—"

"Turn around."

Dobkins turned.

"Bend over."

Dobkins doubled.

Books stuck the pistol under his belt, steadied himself on his left leg, placed the sole of his right boot solidly against the young reporter's fundament.

"Dobkins, you are a prying, pipsqueak, talcum-powder little son of a bitch," he said. "If you ever come dandying around here again, I will kill you."

He shoved with all his strength. Dobkins hurtled through the doorway and across the porch with such momentum that, striking the edge of the top step with head and shoulders, he somersaulted down the flight and tumbled along the wooden sidewalk until he sprawled in a striped heap halfway to the street.

She upbraided him. After the shove, he had gone down on one knee. It was the most savage, most unjustified thing she had ever seen one person do to another, she said, and if she were a man she would horsewhip him for it. Suddenly he reeled up, his face like chalk, and twisted, and fell heavily against a wall. He stood for a moment, head bowed in agony, then put the flat of both hands against the wall to support himself and began, hand by hand, to work his way along the wall in the direction of his room. She feared he might collapse. She came to him and touched his hip as though to assist him. He struck her hand away, muttering that he would tend himself. When he reached the open door he gathered himself, lunged, hands extended, and lowered himself face down upon the bed. She asked if he wanted her to telephone the doctor. He shook his head no.

"Very well," Bond Rogers said. "I'm sure you are in no more discomfort than poor Mr. Dobkins, lying out there on the sidewalk. And if you are, Mr. J. B. Books, it serves you right."

Hostetler found him supine upon the bed, his head pillowed.

"You all right?"

"Yes."

"What happened?"

"I kicked a reporter out of here. It damned near tore me in two."

"Excitation of the cells. You can't do that kind of thing any more, you know."

"I know now. Here, I'll get up."

"No, don't. You lie there and I'll sit by you."

The doctor closed the door behind him and took the armchair by the bed.

"First things first, Doc. I forgot to ask. How much do I owe you?"

Hostetler smiled. "You're a man after my heart, Mr. Books. They usually ask that last, if they do at all. Oh, make it a dollar for the drug and four dollars for the two calls. Don't get up."

"In the closet, in the coat pocket, my wallet. Help yourself."

"I will later." From his bag the physician pulled a book bound in brown leather. "I promised to bring you this. Bruce's *Principles of Surgery*. There's a section on carcinoma you can read if you wish. I've turned down the page corner." He laid it on the library table. "Now." On the table he set a twelve-ounce bottle filled with purplish liquid. "Here you are. Your medicine."

"What is it?"

"Laudanum. A solution of opium in alcohol."

"Opium? Can't that get to be a habit?"

"It can. An addiction, in fact. But in your case—" The doctor shrugged.

Books scowled. "Yes. What's it taste like?"

"Terrible. But there's a consolation. You'll likely have dreams."

"Dreams?"

"Amazing dreams. Perhaps you'll even have visions. Are you much of a reader?"

"No."

"I confess I am, since we're in private. There's an English poet, Coleridge—Samuel Taylor Coleridge. He took opium habitually for a time, as I understand it, and waking one day, wrote down a poem he had composed in his sleep. Based to some extent on the vision he'd had. Quite a phenomenal thing. *Kubla Khan*, it's called. I can recollect the first two lines and the last four. Let me think." Charles Hostetler removed his spectacles and rubbed the bridge of his nose. "Ah, yes, 'In Xanadu did Kubla Khan/ A stately pleasure-dome decree.' "

"Xanadu? Where's that?"

"Who knows? Some strange and oriental sphere of the imagination. Probably in the Near East. Khan must have been some kind of potentate. The last four lines I find unforgettable. 'Weave a circle round him thrice/ And close your eyes with holy dread/ For he on honey-dew hath fed/ And drunk the milk of Paradise.' " He shook his head. "What it means, I'm sure I don't know, but it certainly has a lilt to it."

Books was looking at the laudanum. "The milk of Paradise—at least there's alcohol in it. What's the stuff for?"

"It's the most potent painkiller we have."

"Oh. How much do I take?"

"As much as you need. When you need it. Prescribe for yourself. A spoonful should do you at first."

"Later?"

Hostetler put on his spectacles. "You'll require

more and more. It will have less and less effect, I'm afraid."

The two men were silent. A dwindle of sunlight touched the bottle on the table between them, refracting a purple image upward onto the crystalline lampshade, where it nested raucously among the blue, brown, and green birds of paradise. The silence was one of mutual reticence. Books did not care to ask, Hostetler had no desire to respond. So they waited, each for the other. It was the doctor who broke a path, even though oblique, for both of them.

"I haven't much of a bedside manner," he admitted. "Never have had. In a case like yours, I'm damned if I can be cheery. And poetry's no help."

"You're sure it's cancer."

"Unquestionably. I wish I could do more, Books, but I can't. Someday we'll lay the monster low, I'd bet on it, but that's in the future, probably long after I'm gone myself. The present is where we are now."

Books unbuttoned the collar of his shirt. "You said last time I can still be up and about a while yet. For how long?"

"I don't know. But you will. One morning you'll wake and say to yourself, 'I can't go out any more. I couldn't even dress myself. Here I am, in this bed, and here I'll stay.' "

They were silent again.

"God damn it," Books said.

"Yes. God damn it," said Hostetler.

"A hell of a way to go," Books said.

"A hell of a way to go," said Hostetler.

Books laid a hand on the *Principles of Surgery,*

then withdrew it. "You told me it would be a hard death. How hard?"

The physician closed his bag, stepped to the closet, reached inside for the coat, and brought out a wallet. "How much did I say? Five?"

"All right, Doc. How hard?"

"Five, yes. Beware of morbidity." He replaced the wallet and pulled the curtain.

"I want to know, Hostetler. What will happen to me?"

Hostetler tucked away his own wallet, came behind the leather chair, and picking up his bag, placing it in the seat, put both hands on the back. He was a short, stoutish man of sixty or so, with short gray hair and benign blue eyes. "Unless you insist, I'd rather not talk about it."

"I insist."

Hostetler pursed his lips. "You will waste away. The process will be slow at first, then rapid."

"Waste away?"

"Loss of flesh. Known as 'cachexia.' "

"What else?"

"The bones of the face become prominent. The skin takes on a grayish cast. You will be a pretty awful sight. No one will dare tell you, but you will. Pretty awful."

"What else?"

"There will be increasing severity of pain. In the lumbar spine, in the hips and groins."

"What else?"

"Must we go on?"

"Yes."

"Your water will shut off progressively. The bladder will swell because you can't unload it. You will gradually become uremic. Poisoned by your own waste products, due to a failure of the kidneys."

"That all?"

"By this time the agony will be unbearable, and no drug will moderate it. Hopefully, you will become comatose. Until you do, you will scream."

"Jesus Christ."

Charles Hostetler picked up his bag, walked to the door. His look for the first time was severe, almost angry. "I regret you forced me to be specific, Mr. Books. If you need me, telephone. Good day, sir."

He banged the door behind him. He opened it again at once, re-entered, and closed the door apologetically. "I'm sorry I was short with you. There's just one more thing I'll say. If you stop to think about it, we have considerable in common. Both of us have a lot to do with death. I stave it off when I can. You inflict it when you have to. I am not a brave man, but you must be, by virtue of your avocation. Well, you can be braver now than you have ever been, and it won't help you a tinker's damn. This is not advice, not even a suggestion, just something to reflect upon while your mind is still clear." He studied his shoe tops for a moment. "If I were in your circumstances, I know what I would not do."

"What?"

Charles Hostetler listened, as though to take care he were not overheard. "I won't put it in so many words. It runs counter to the ethics of my profession. But I would not die a death such as I have just described."

"No?"

"I would not. Not if I had your courage. I would not. And especially your skill with weapons."

Books stared at him.

"Good-by."

Books stared at him. "Thank you."

That night he could not sleep for pain. He got out of bed, pulled on the lamp, sat down on his pillow, picked up the book Hostetler had brought, and examined the title page. The author of *Principles of Surgery* was "James W. D. Bruce, Professor of Surgery in the University of Edinburgh; Surgeon to the Royal Infirmary." The volume had been published in Philadelphia by Lea and Blanchard in 1878.

He found the turned-down page corner and opened the book to the section headed "Carcinoma." He read the author's definition: *"This is the occult malignant tumour, whose open condition is termed* Cancer." He continued to read, slowly, until he came to this passage, and finished it:

The cachectic state of system becomes more and more aggravated; sleep is gone; appetite fails; emaciation is great, and still increasing; the sallow, wan, cadaverous expression of face becomes more marked; the whole frame grows bloodless; a malignant hectic, as it may be termed, is established; and life is gradually exhausted, in much physical misery.

He slapped the book shut. He could read no more of it. But something, the shutting perhaps, caused an access of pain so excruciating that he sat forward, fists on forehead, and rocked himself.

When he opened his eyes he saw the bottle on the table. What was it Hostetler had said? A spoonful should do him at first? He reached for it, uncapped, tipped, and swallowed what he judged was a spoonful of the laudanum. It had a bitter taste. He capped the bottle, replaced it, sat back, waited. Relief came within minutes. It was not so much a cessation of pain as an overture, warm and seductive, throughout his pelvic region, of insensitivity—this accompanied at the same time by a slow flood of euphoria. He was laved, as though by pleasure. He rose from the chair easily, without discomfort, for the first time in two months. He grinned like a boy.

He pulled out the light, got back into bed, settled himself, grinned again, and slept.

He dreamed. He did not have a vision. He dreamed of the gunfight in the restaurant in Bisbee, Arizona, the only scrap in which he had ever been wounded. The two men who had thrown down on him, the men he had killed, were faceless now; he had never seen them before that night, when they had earlier exchanged insults with him at a monte table in a saloon. He had not even known their names. But it had not been either of them who hit him, it had been a third party, a complete stranger, a drunk, a spectator as uninvolved as a spider on the ceiling, who lurched up from a table and a meal and drew and felled Books with a bullet in the belly and walked out of the restaurant picking his teeth. Books had long ago learned that the outcome of most gunplay was unpredictable. Too often, when weapons were pulled and working, it was not the principals who had their way. It was some nobody, some butt-in with a secret compulsion to use a gun once in his life on another human being or to die spectacularly, some six-fingered bastard who couldn't when sober hit a cow in the teats with a tin cup, who rushed from the wings and directed the last incalculable act of the drama. Bat Masterson had said you had to have guts, proficiency with firearms, and deliberation. In short, you had to be professional. He hadn't mentioned the eye you had to have in the back of your head for the dumb-ass amateur. But then, Masterson had always been full of shit.

He dreamed, too, of Serepta, of making love to her and of the sound which issued from her open mouth as she neared her coming. It was like the mourning of a dove at first, an elegy for youth and strength and beauty being spent, and in the spending being lost forever; then swiftening, rising in pitch and power as she achieved orgasm, it was as though her heart were in her mouth, pulsing a song of life for him, an ululation at once tragic and exultant: la, la, la, la, la, la, la. He had never heard another woman make such a sound in sex.

He woke him.

Pain woke him.

He pulled on the lamp and squinted at his watch. The laudanum had given him almost four hours.

"You'll need more and more," Hostetler had said. "It will have less and less effect."

He debated hitting the purple bottle again, decided against it.

He thought: That was a peculiar thing, Hostetler saying it before I thought of it. I would have later, probably, but I am glad he did now. There is nothing yellow about it. It makes good sense. A man is a fool to die slow if he does not have to. And I will know when to do it, too, Hostetler said I would. There will come a day. On that day I will take care of it. I am damned if John Bernard Books will go screaming.

He put his right hand on the congenial steel of the gun under his pillow, his left on that of the one at his side under the covers. He had slept with his guns for years. He wondered which of them he would use.

Books thought: No matter.

He thought: Both are friends of mine.

# Three

Jack Pulford ran the faro layout at Keating's, one of the ninety-six saloons in El Paso. He was noted for his toilet and his skill with a revolver. A singularly handsome blond man of forty or so, he was shaved by a barber, and since his hands, as he said, were the tools of his trade, and the dealing of faro required that they be on constant display, he also had the barber trim and buff his fingernails. He wore a low-cut linen vest and a clean white silk shirt every day. The shirt was set with diamond studs. He carried a small .38-caliber Smith & Wesson in an unobtrusive but businesslike holster high and handy on his right hip. Pulford was acknowledged the best pistol shot in west Texas. He could draw and fire with astonishing rapidity and accuracy, and practiced often with targets before an admiring audience on the town baseball field. It was gossiped that he had killed a man in Abilene, and a deputy sheriff in Lander, Wyoming, and although neither killing could be verified locally, they were fact.

One exploit, however, on a February night in 1899, had gilt-edged his status in El Paso. Dealing faro then at the Gem, handling both the case and cage himself, he had been accused of bracing the deck by a man named Cleo James. Pulford slapped James twice, returned his losses, and had him ejected. James took his grudge elsewhere, embellished it with liquor, obtained a gun, returned to the Gem, and began firing at Pulford as he entered the front door, much to the dismay of the clientele. It was an error of judgment compounded by the distance between him and his target. Pulford sat in the back room, the gambling room, of the saloon, framed by the doorway. James had fired four shots at him by the time the gambler rose, drew, aimed, and killed him with a single round through the heart. A bull's-eye at such long range, and under fire, was incredible. A tape measure was produced. Between the place where James fell and Pulford fired, the measure was eighty-four feet, three inches.

He was presiding at the table one night in late January, two years later, when one of the players remarked that J. B. Books was in town, holed up in a boardinghouse on Overland. But everyone knew. The game continued. And very bad off the player added, very bad off. Dying of a cancer.

That stopped the game. The informant was closely questioned. He had it on the best authority. He'd heard it from a friend who'd heard it from Thibido himself, the marshal. Books was cashing in.

For some reason everyone glanced at Jack Pulford. "That's hard news," he said, studying the sheen of his fingernails. "There was a man I could've beat."

No one at the table doubted him out loud.

He had been taking laudanum only at night, two spoonfuls, one at bedtime, one four hours later.

This afternoon the pain would not allow him to wait until bedtime. It was his first dose during the afternoon.

Relieved at once, he picked up his newspaper and began to read an article headed THE BLOOMERITE OF '01:

There is much discussion going on now in regard to woman's dress on the bicycle. A New York writer furnishes the following on the bloomer question. It's a hard question to answer. A year ago women who blushed at the mere mention of bloomers now wear them gladly, defiantly, and gracefully. True, the bloomers are almost as voluminous as skirts, but at any place frequented by women cyclists about the metropolitan district it is quite apparent that the bloomers are shrinking slowly but surely. Women talk now of the full bloomer, the three-quarter bloomer, and the half-bloomer. When the fractions get a trifle smaller, the bloomer will have shrunk into tight-fitting knickerbockers.

Black satin bloomers are a common sight on the great Brooklyn bicycle road running to Coney Island. As a matter of fact, the bloomer habit is much stronger in quiet Brooklyn than in dashing New York. Perhaps it is because. . .

"Come in."

Bond Rogers had knocked. "Mr. Books."

"Mrs. Rogers. What is your opinion of bloomers?"

"I beg your pardon!"

He rustled his newspaper. "I was reading about them. They have become the rage in New York

City. It says that women who blushed at the mention of them a year ago now wear them 'gladly, defiantly, and gracefully.' "

She had gone as crimson as his pillow. "I came to see—" she began. "What was it? Oh yes, what you can eat. I mean, if you can have what I'm serving tonight."

"No, you didn't."

"I wish you would stop contradicting me."

"I wish you would say what you mean."

"Very well. I'm sorry about the other day, after Mr. Dobkins left. The reporter."

"After I kicked him out."

"I apologize for my lecture. It was probably unchristian of me. And also my breaking down when you told me of your—your affliction. I'm sorry. I realize no one else would take you in. So I wanted to say, I will do whatever I can for you."

"Thank you. I can eat anything. I am sorry myself that I struck your hand away. I guaranteed not to be a burden to you, and I have been too proud, most of my life, to take help from anybody. I will have to learn. Do sit down a minute."

"Well."

"Please do."

She took the straight chair. "Is the doctor sure? That you have cancer?"

"He is."

"Isn't there anything he can do?"

Books indicated the purple bottle. "He gave me that. It's a painkiller—laudanum."

"Laudanum? Isn't that habit-forming?"

"So?"

She realized. "Oh. Yes, How silly of me."

He considered her. "Mrs. Rogers, are you afraid of me?"

"Yes."

"Why?"

"Those guns in the closet. What you've done with them. The kind of man you are."

"Up to two months ago you'd have had every right to be. Afraid. A lot of people have been. But not now."

"I hope not."

"You may have been afraid of too much," he said. "Widows sometimes are, women alone. My being here will help you get over that. Maybe I will be good for you."

"Good for me?"

"Yes. I have never been afraid of anything. Cautious, yes, but that's different. Maybe I can bring out the spunk in you. I'm sure it is there."

The turn of the conversation disquieted her. She rose quickly. "I must get started with supper." She moved toward the door.

Since her back was turned, and she could not see the effort it required, he hauled himself upright. "Before you go, Mrs. Rogers, there's a favor I'd like to ask. I have been in this room too long. I wondered if you would go for a drive in the country with me tomorrow morning. I will hire a hack."

"Tomorrow? Oh, I couldn't, Mr. Books, thank you just the same. Don't you know about tomorrow?"

"No."

"President McKinley will be in El Paso. There's to be a parade, the McGinty Band will play, and all the school children are to march, carrying flags. He's expected to speak in the plaza. I couldn't miss that."

He leaned on the back of the armchair. "Are you sure that is your reason?"

"I certainly am."

"I wish you would reconsider. If there is a big shindig downtown, that's fine. We can skin out of town with no one the wiser. I do not care to be seen. Just for an hour or two?"

"Mr. Books, I appreciate—"

"You don't care to be alone with me. O.K., have your boy come along for a chaperon."

"It isn't that, I assure you. I've been widowed only a year. People would—"

"People." He scowled. "Ma'am, if I have to work on your sympathy, I will. This may be the last chance I will have. Doc Hostetler says there will come a day when I can't get out of bed. Before that day I want to see the world again—the skies and spaces—and I do not fancy seeing it alone. I have been full of alone lately. All we have done, you and I, since I moved in here, is scratch at each other, and then apologize. Well, if I am going to die in your house, I think we should try to be friends. So I wish like hell you would go with me. I apologize for the language."

Bond Rogers had not imagined he had that many words in him, or that much eloquence. It was true: under the menace, below the profanity, at the end of the fuse of violence which smoldered always, was the child with a stubbed toe who needed comforting. She had come upon that child in Ray, although the qualities which obscured it were kindly in his instance rather than reprehensible. Behind her husband's smiling face was a soul. Under this man's coat there were guns. She wished with all her heart that she had loved Ray more while she had him, and let him know it. For suddenly it was too late, he was gone forever. This man, awaiting grimly her response, would decline day by day, but die he would, just as surely as Ray, and much more terribly, and under her roof, too. It seemed to her that she must not make the same mistake twice. She feared what Books was, she despised what he had been, but she had taken him into her house and permitted him to remain when he had informed her almost casually that his case was hopeless; the least she could do in his last days, then, was to extend a kind though decorous hand. She searched for a text, and found it. "And the greatest of these," she sermonized herself, "is Charity."

"I will go with you," she said.

"Capital." It was the first genuine smile she had seen on his face. "Let's make it ten o'clock. Just for an hour or two. Invite your son along. And will you ask him to trot down to the livery in the morning and bring us a rig?"

"Yes," she said.

"I am very much obliged," he said.

She decided to test Gillom. She had not been invited anywhere by a man for a year. His reaction might reveal something she should know.

She told him, but he was inscrutable. He said that was swell. She learned nothing.

Then she added that he was invited too. His face lit up like a fiesta. He smacked a palm with a fist. "Hot damn!"

"You'll miss seeing the President."

"Who cares? How many men's McKinley killed?"

"I scarcely—"

"J. B. Books and us! Gosh, Ma, d'you think he'll bring his guns along?"

"I hope not."

"What if somebody sees him that hates him? What if there's a shoot-out and we're in on it?" Gillom crouched, drew, and fired his finger. "Bing! Bang! Bango!"

What his mother learned about her son was not what she had expected to.

At ten o'clock Books donned his vest and frock coat, which was tailor-made in the Prince Albert mode but single-breasted rather than double, so that he had quick entry to his vest, adjusted his Stetson, started, then returned for a spoonful of laudanum. He had determined to leave his pillow but, given the torment his rump would be sure to take in a gig or a buckboard, he did not believe he could do without the intercession of the drug. It was his first morning dose, though he relied on it afternoons now, as well as nights.

Mrs. Rogers waited for him on the porch. He took her arm. Gillom Rogers waited behind a team on the front seat of a phaeton—not a gig or a buckboard but a phaeton—a black four-wheeled, spring-seated, gilt-spoked, folding-tip equipage fit for a king or a president or the madam of a high-priced parlor house.

"Mighty stylish," Books commented.

"I didn't think you ought to ride in any old hack, Mister Books. Mose Tarrant had to dust this one off. He says he don't rent it too often, except for funerals. Hop in, ladies and gents!"

"Keep to the back streets," said Books.

"Yes, sir."

Books opened the door, seated his landlady and himself in the rear. Gillom took the reins and clucked. The team stepped out smartly.

Their way was eastward. The streets were empty, for most of El Paso's populace and traffic had gravitated to the plaza for the McKinley parade and speechifying. Brass music drifted down the hollow thoroughfares. Between closed and shuttered stores the drumbeats loitered. Gillom chauffeured them north and, as the political discord faded, followed San Antonio Street out of town along the valley of the Rio Grande.

It was a drear day. Under a gray sky, under an impassive mountain, under a crow which accompanied it for a time, the phaeton rolled, the only sounds the inquiry of the crow, a grit of pebbles, a creak of harness, the snort and footfall of the team at a trot. Weather in west Texas this time of year depended on the whim or wind. When it came down the pass from the north as now, snow was not uncommon, though transient, but an immigrant wind from the south, from Old Mexico or the Gulf, turned the valley tropical overnight, drenching it often with rain and bloating the river into flood. When either of these winds desisted the hours were dry, the sun shone, the air glittered.

In the front seat, his jacket collar up against the chill, Gillom tended to his knitting. Books asked his guest if she wished the top raised. She did not, thank you. She was protected by an ankle-length coat, her head and shoulders by a shawl of black wool.

They dusted through Ysleta, a huddle of small adobe houses and a church with a broken cross. Children with brown and ancient eyes stared after them, and starving dogs gave chase. Then they were out under the gray sky again, into the silence and the long, long valley. They passed between vineyards, the vines sere and leafless, between barrens of stub corn and the winter tatter of squash and beans and melons. They saw a yoke of oxen in the distance, plodding toward the edges of the world.

Books leaned forward, pointed at a line of cottonwoods. His driver nodded, reined the team off the road and into a field and to a stop alongside an *acequia*, or irrigation ditch. He gangled down, tied the team, and opening the rear door, bowed low.

"Time to stretch your legs, folks."

His passengers alighted. From a pocket he slipped a pint bottle, offered it to Books. "Time to grease your tonsils, too."

"Gillom Rogers! Is that whiskey?" demanded his mother.

"Heck, no, Ma. Tiger milk."

Books accepted the bottle. "Do you want him to have this?" he asked her.

"I do not."

Books put it away in a pocket of his coat. "Take a walk, son."

Gillom chewed a lip. "Don't call me son, Mr. Books. I have a name."

"Take a walk, Gillom."

The youth looked at one, then the other, grinned as though he knew a secret, and left them, traipsing down the ditch.

Books took Bond Rogers' arm and walked with her along the *acequia*. The water was swift and clear, a gift from the Rio Grande and the law of gravity. The cottonwoods which lined it were immense, a hundred years old, and the leaves were winter gold.

"He needs a father, and a woodshed, and a strap," said Books. "Why don't you marry again?"

"Are you feeling all right?"

"As well as can be. Why don't you marry again?"

"That is none of your affair."

"I do not have time to be polite."

"Very well. I haven't been asked, for one thing. For another, I loved my husband and still do."

"Why?"

"I can't count the reasons. He was splendid with Gillom, for example. They went to ballgames, fishing, to bullfights over in Ciudad Juárez, everywhere together. Ray played cornet in the McGinty Band, and Gillom would sit through every concert."

"Ray. What did he die of?"

"A stroke, they think. He simply failed to come home for supper one evening. They found him slumped at his desk."

"He was lucky."

"No. He was forty-one."

Books strolled thoughtfully at her side, hands clasped behind his back. "Did he leave you much?"

"Just the house, which we built. By means of a large loan at the bank. And Gillom, of course."

"He worries you."

"You noticed. He certainly does. He refuses to attend school, preferring to hang around Utah Street. Today is the first time I've seen him with whiskey, but I'm sure he drinks when he can. He curses. He has stolen from my purse. He comes in at all hours and won't account to me. If his father were here it would be different, but he isn't."

"Why do you say that?"

"Woman's intuition. Male logic. He loved Ray deeply. Now he hates him for dying and hates me for living. He even hates himself, I suspect—I'm not clear why. Perhaps he thinks he must be the man of the family now, and fears he may not be man enough, and therefore must prove it." She stopped. "How I grieve for him. He bears a grudge against God, I guess. I can't reason with him—all I can do is mother him, and he doesn't want that."

Books had halted. "You could give him another father."

"Who? One like you? So he could be taught how to handle a gun and murder and carouse? Oh, he respects you all right—he's in absolute awe of you. He'd shine your boots if you asked." Her tone grew harsh. "Oh no, thank you, J. B. Books! Don't you dare be his dime-novel hero! Don't you dare let him love you and respect you the way he did his father—ever! You've not worthy of it!"

She glared at him. Books scowled at her, then put hands behind back and resumed their promenade. "Can't you send him away?"

She caught up. "On the next train if I could. El Paso's no place to rear a boy, especially if one is alone. I have a cousin in Massachusetts, and near her there's a private school, the Milton Academy. I'd give anything to send him there for a year or two—but five hundred dollars might as well be the moon." She tightened her shawl about her. "Let's leave the subject. Please enjoy your outing. Why should you care about us anyway, Gillom and me? You have concerns enough of your own."

He turned to one of the cottonwoods and put his back to it comfortably, letting the trunk take his weight. He said, "I have no one else to care about."

The statement disarmed her. She joined him, leaning herself against the trunk, which was five feet in diameter. These trees had great gnarled roots twisting down into the *acequia*, stealing from it in all seasons their stature and endurance.

"Are you married?" she asked.

"No. I was once. I was eighteen. She died, trying to have a girl. So did the child."

"I'm sorry. You should have married again. The right woman might have changed the course of your life."

"I doubt it. I have a sudden nature."

"It's my turn to pry. How long have you been— been a gun man? Perhaps I should use the term the paper did the other morning—it has so much more dignity—a 'shootist'?"

"I don't think of myself as either."

"You don't? Well, if not, what are you?"

"I have earned a living several ways. I speculated in cotton, down in Louisiana. I bought and sold cattle once, at the railhead in Kansas. I struck a little gold. I have made a good deal at cards over the years, and lost a good deal, too. In general, I have had a damned good time. Till lately."

"Lately, yes. Have you relatives?"

"I used to have, over in San Saba County. I don't know where they are."

"What about friends?"

"No."

"None at all?"

"I have always herded by myself."

"Do you mean no one will come to see you? Or people you'll want to send word to, that you are—"

"Going to perdition? No."

"I'm shocked. I pity you, truly. To have no one now—that is indeed a tragedy."

"Here comes Gillom."

He dawdled toward them, pitching stones into the ditch.

"What does 'J. B.' stand for?" she asked quickly.

"John Bernard. What is yours?"

"Bond."

"Pleased to make your acquaintance, Bond."

"How do you do."

He moved away from the tree to meet Gillom. To her surprise she noted, when they met, that her son was taller than Books. She had never looked at the man-killer that way. She had equated notoriety with height. Suddenly she saw a pistol in his hand.

"Ever fired one of these?" Books asked Gillom.

"A couple times. A guy I know, name of Cobb, let me fire his Colt's. He's got two beauties."

"Want to try this one?"

"Gee, do I!"

"All right." Books pointed. "See the knot in that trunk yonder? It's about sixty feet away. Stand, aim, and fire five rounds. Easy when you pull. It's a hair trigger."

"Why not six?"

"You keep the hammer chamber empty. An extra safety. Never load six unless you're sure you will be using the weapon."

"Oh. Why such a short barrel?"

"Speed."

"Oh. O.K. Ma'll have a conniption, though." Gillom took the Remington, faced the cottonwood, raised his right arm, aimed. "There's no sight!"

"Close in, you don't need one. Steady now. Take your time. Pull easy."

Gillom fired five times, slowly, re-aiming after each round. The shots were muffled by leaves and the lowering sky, and fell like a single syllable upon the ear despite the intervals between rounds, for the echo of one explosion was fused with the explosion of the next round. Through a haze of powder smoke the youth turned, his expression one of such wonder, such ecstasy, that it was almost grotesque, to find Books with a second pistol in hand, a few feet away, aiming at a knot in the tree adjacent to his own target.

The man fired five times, even more deliberately, and lowered his arm.

Gillom jumped to him, returned his weapon, then dashed to examine the two knots while Books reloaded immediately from a box of bullets.

"My spread's no bigger'n yours! Hey, damn if I didn't tie you! Hey, look, Ma!" Gillom whooped. "I tied 'im! Look!"

She had not moved, did not move.

Books put the guns away inside his coat. He appeared disinterested in his marksmanship. Together they walked back to Bond Rogers. Gillom strutted.

When they approached, her lips were a thin, stern line. "Why did you do it?" she accused the man.

"A weapon wants firing regularly. Otherwise it fouls when you need it."

"You mean, the main purpose of this drive was to shoot those guns?"

"That was one. I had others."

"I want to go home," she said. "Now."

"If you wish. Here."

He gave Gillom the pint bottle. Gillom winked at

him, grinned at his mother, and shoved it in his jacket.

Bond Rogers' fingers worked the wool of her shawl in frustration. Striding to the phaeton, she opened the rear door herself, seated herself. Books joined her. Gillom untied the team and climbed aboard. Instead of taking the reins, however, he stepped up and sat facing his passengers on the top of the front seat. Just then the gray sky above them was slit by a knife of blue, and such was the position of the sun behind the ceiling of cloud that the vehicle and its occupants were encompassed by light. It was a phenomenon.

Gillom gazed at the gun man as does a pup its master. "Mr. Books, how many men have you killed?"

"Gillom, you have no right to ask that," his mother rebuked.

Books considered his questioner. "I disremember," he said.

"How could you kill so many?"

"Gillom!"

"Everybody has laws he lives by, I expect. I have mine as well."

"What laws?"

Bond Rogers was dismayed. Yet she waited, evidently as curious as her son.

"I will not be laid a hand on. I will not be wronged. I will not stand for an insult. I don't do these things to others. I require the same from them."

To untangle his tongue, Gillom made a face. "What I meant was, how could you get into so many fights and always come out on top? I tied you."

"I had to," said Books. "It isn't being fast, it is whether or not you're willing. The difference is, when it comes down to it, most men are not willing. I found that out early. They will blink an eye, or take a breath, before they pull a trigger. I won't."

As miraculously as the sky had opened, it was sealed, and the three sat once more in chill and shade. A wind mourned through the dry leaves of the cottonwoods. The team stomped, restive.

"Do you regret the life you've lived, Mr. Books?" the woman asked.

He looked a hole through Gillom. "I regret I quit school too soon. And frittered away my young years in bad company. At that age, I was too big for my britches."

"I was thinking of your victims."

"Mrs. Rogers, I have never killed a good man."

"How do you know? It's the Lord who should judge, surely, not weak, mortal creatures like us."

Books lay back against the leather. He seemed weary. "From my observation, ma'am, the Lord has not made a very damned good job of it. Let me put an individual at the business end of a gun and I will judge as well as He can."

That evening he perused his newspaper. He noted two items in particular, the first in the humor column:

"Last night, when I accepted Harry," said Miss Stockson Bonds, who was suspicious as well as homely, "he kissed me on the forehead."

"The idea!" exclaimed Miss Pepprey.

"I wonder why he didn't kiss me on the

lips," said Miss Stockson Bonds. "Oh, horrors! Probably he had been drinking!"

"Very likely," said Miss Pepprey. "That is, if he proposed to you."

The drive into the valley and the tensions between mother, son, and himself, strung as taut between the three as telephone wires, had worn him into the bone. Pain made the paper rustle in his fingers. He had had to take two doses of laudanum since their return, and he could wait no longer for another. He took a spoonful.

The second item was an advertisement:

Yes, August Flower has the largest sale of any medicine in the civilized world. Your mothers and grandmothers never thought of using anything else for Indigestion or Biliousness, Doctors were scarce, and they seldom heard of Appendicitis, Nervous Prostration or Heart Failure. They used August Flower to clean out the system and stop fermentation of undigested food, regulate the action of the liver, and stimulate the nerves, and that is all they took when feeling dull and bad with headaches and other aches. You only need a few doses of Green's August Flower, in liquid form, to make you satisfied that there is nothing seriously the matter with you!

He stripped to his longjohns, used the slop-jar, opened the windows, pulled out the lamp, and got into bed, pearl-handled Remington under the covers, black under his pillow.

\*        \*        \*

Pain woke him at one o'clock. The analgesic effect of the laudanum was of shorter duration now. He had another spoonful, and slept again.

He woke again just after four in the morning. this was a new agony. It was as though two iron screws were being rotated inch by inch into his pelvic region, laterally, from hip to hip, and upward, from genitals to navel. In too much haste for the spoon, he tilted the bottle. Pressure on his bladder would have roused him in any event. Taking the slop-jar from under the bed, he squatted over it and waited for relief. Frequently, such was the state of his plumbing, he had to wait three or four minutes to achieve flow.

He closed his eyes, conjecturing drowsily whether or not he had made a mistake after all, allowing Gillom Rogers, to target-practice with one of the guns the day before. At a certain age, boys fell in love with firearms more readily than with girls. Some of them never recovered.

He opened his eyes. They sent to his brain the impression of a shadow upon the lace curtain of the window at the south. His brain resisted the impression. It was four in the morning. The moon would have declined. He squinted.

The shadow moved.

Books did likewise.

Deliberately, without waste motion, and soundlessly, he lifted the slop-jar to a place between the library table and the armchair, out of the way.

Kneeling by the bed, he bunched the sheet and blankets lengthwise and eased the black-handled pistol from beneath the pillow.

As he let himself down by the bed onto his back, one hand on the frame under the mattress, gun in the other, he became conscious of a second shadow, this one in the curtain folds of the western window. So there were two of them.

He crabbed himself under the bed—not at the center, under the bunched covers, but at the side. The fingers of his left hand clenched the frame.

The curtains at the south window were parted by the head and shoulders of a man. He hesitated, adjusting his vision.

Extending his arm, the intruder fired four rounds into what resembled a sleeping figure in the center of the bed. After the last he climbed rapidly over the sill into the room.

Simultaneously, there was a gunflash through the west window and, having fired, the second assailant propelled himself through it with such awkward force that he tore the curtain from the wall.

Standing over the bed, the first man let go a fifth, an insurance, round into the bunched covers.

In close confines, the reports were like detonations. The floor of the room seemed to heave. The walls of the room hurled thunder at each other. Six rounds had been fired within twenty seconds, five by the man who had entered through the south window, one by the man through the west. Books had counted.

Using his left arm, levering his upper body into the open like a reptile striking from a crevice, he fired twice at the man to his left, the west, heard the smack of lead into flesh, then recoiled below.

The man grunted, fell backward, shrouded in lace, crashing against the washbowl to the floor.

Still crouched over the bed, the first intruder

fired at Books's gunflash, and the bullet splintered
a corner of the library table.

Instantly, levering himself even with the upper
edge of the mattress, Books fired once at him. He
staggered backward to the wall, dropped his empty
weapon.

"Don't kill me, Books, oh Christ don't kill me!"
he screamed. "I'm shot out!"

Books came cautiously to his knees.

There was ample light now. The bunched bed-
covers were on fire.

Through the flames, Books watched the wounded
man crawl toward the south window, flop himself
on his elbows over the sill in the crazed hope he
could fall out of the house to safety.

"I'm gutshot, Books!" he yelled. "Jesus Christ,
don't murder me!"

Raising the Remington over the blazing bed-
clothes, Books sighted on his enemy's rectum.

"You tried to kill me," he said hoarsely "So
long, you murdering son of a bitch."

He fired. Ranging half the length of the spine,
shattering vertebrae and destroying the central nervous system, the .44 slug drove the body halfway
through the window.

Books placed his weapon on the carpet.

Twisting then, he reached, got a grip on the rim
of the slop-jar, lifted it high, swung, and doused
the flaming bed with urine.

The door of the room burst open.

A stench sickened them. Black powder smoke
blinded them.

One of the railroad men, a gnome in a night-
shirt, balding and elderly, with watering eyes and

hairy ankles, edged tentatively into the room and turned on the ceiling fixture.

At the door, the other railroad man, the middle-aged schoolteacher, Bond Rogers, and her son Gillom drew incredulous breath.

J. B. Books sat beside the bed in his underwear. He stared vacantly, not at them but at a wall patterned with sprays of blue and golden lilies.

Below the mirror and washbowl, both of which were bloodspattered, a dead man lay on his back, a revolver in his hand, his mouth open, his winding sheet a web of torn curtains.

A foul steam rose from the blackened stew of the bed.

Another man seemed to be attempting to climb out of the south window, out of the house. But he was still, his legs spraddled wide. And from between his buttocks, through the denim of his pants, a dark stream welled as though he were excreting blood.

To wake from a sleep of peace, to look into that infernal room, to outrage the nostrils with the odors of terror and death and madness therein, was to have a presentiment of Hell itself. Those witness at the door stood as though nailed to the floor. The railroad men turned heads. The schoolteacher tried to shriek and, unable, commenced to wail.

"Telephone the marshal, Mrs. Rogers," ordered Books. "The rest of you, get the hell out of here."

In flannel dressing gown she waited in the parlor for the marshal. Gillom could not sit. She had even had to remind him to put on his trousers. Barefoot, he paced up and down before her.

"God," he said.

He ran a hand through his rat's-nest hair.

"God!"

He swept a toe along the fringe at the base of the sofa.

"God, Ma, did you see that? That's the way it happens, Ma—the real thing! My God, he got both of 'em! They must've come through the windows, guns going, and he's so fast, he killed 'em both! You wait—half this town'll be coming by our house every day for a week, gawping and pointing! Will we ever be in the papers, too! J. B. Books in a shoot-out right in our house—we can brag on this the rest of our lives!"

She had never seen him so excited. His face, his eyes, were feverish. And suddenly she hated her son. Her home, the home she and Ray had dreamed of and saved for, had been desecrated. If her departed husband knew, and she had no doubt he did, he could not in an eternity forgive her. And she hated Books. She had let a killer into her house, let him buy her forbearance and charity and the adoration of her boy for the pottage of four dollars a day. She remembered them together yesterday, Gillom as tall as the gun man, shooting at tree trunks, competing yet sharing in a false and deadly virility. She shuddered again to explosions and yells. A viper of revenge entered her bosom.

"You respect him, don't you, Gillom?"

"Wouldn't you?"

"You worship the ground he walks on, don't you?"

"Damn right I do!"

"You think as much of him as you did of your father, don't you?"

That brought him up short.

"Don't you?"

"I told you, Ma. Don't talk—"

"He's dying," said Bond Rogers.

"Who?"

"J. B. Books."

"Hah."

"Of natural causes. He told me the other day. That's why Doctor Hostetler has been here twice. He has a cancer."

"I don't believe it."

"It's only a matter of time—several weeks perhaps. That's why he wanted to go for a drive yesterday. He said it would be his last opportunity to see the world."

"You're lying."

"Have I ever?"

"He'd have told me. He likes me a lot."

"He's dying, Gillom."

He understood at last. He believed at last. She could have cut out her tongue. For his reaction was as startling, and as frightening, as a shot in the dark of night.

Gillom turned his back on her. A string of reserve was pulled in him. He sank awkwardly to his knees and buried his face in the seat of a chair. He sobbed. He stained with his tears the velours of the chair, an overstuffed of which she was particularly choice. His hands tore the antimacassars from the arms. He cried as desperately as he had at another bereavement.

She had wanted to hurt him, her own flesh, and hence to do herself injury—but not to this terrible extent. She had hated him momentarily, and hated Books. Gillom would hate her now, and Books, too, and have in time his own vengeance. If the man in the corner room had taken life tonight, she was guilty of a sin almost as grave. Given the secret of death to keep, she had used it instead as a weapon, and by means of it on impulse she had robbed a seventeen-year-old of hope. On the slate of his future, she knew now, Gillom had begun to chalk a new image, and with one cruel stroke she had wiped the slate blank.

In a cold dawn, in a cold house, Bond Rogers sat, watching through her own tears her son grieve the loss, in less than two years, of two fathers.

"Who were they?"

"Ben Shoup, the one you shot in the ass."

"Shoup."

"The other name of Norton. Two no-goods, not from around here. Know them?"

"I recollect the name Shoup back in San Saba County when I was a kid. I had family there."

"Well, they knew you. And I knew sure as death and taxes we were due for something like this." Thibido sipped from his coffee cup. "Came in the windows, did they? How'd you manage?"

"I was up taking a leak. I stayed under the bed till I placed them, then came out shooting."

"Just like that, two more notches." The marshal glanced at the blood-blotched mirror and wash-bowl, and at the dried rivulet in the carpet under the south window. He shook his head in disgust. "Place looks like a damned slaughterhouse. Smells like it, too."

"They must have heard I was hanging up my irons for good. Figured I couldn't defend myself."

"They found out."

Books considered him. "Only three people knew—

Doc Hostetler, the landlady, and you. How would you guess the word got around?"

"Not from me," lied Thibido quickly. "My profession, you learn to keep your eyes skinned and your mouth shut."

"Mine too," said Books.

They drank the coffee Mrs. Rogers had brought them. It was six o'clock in the morning. Several of Thibido's deputies had arrived with him and removed the bodies. The landlady had stripped the bed, and taking the sheets and blankets into the back yard, burned them, but the stink lingered in the room.

"Goddam fools," Thibido reflected.

"Who?"

"Shoup, Norton. All they had to do was hold their face and hands and you'd be in a wooden box and they'd of had the last laugh. How long now, Books?"

"I don't know."

"What's the doc say?"

"He doesn't."

Thibido smiled. "How you feeling? A little more poorly every day?"

"That's damned unkind of you."

"It was damned unkind of you to come to El Paso to kick the bucket." Walter Thibido tilted his chair and made himself comfortable. "I blame myself for this hash. I should of badged some good men and tied your legs under a burro and hurrahed you out of town the day you showed—but I didn't. I shed a tear, I sweet-talked Mrs. Rogers into letting you stay, I guaranteed her you wouldn't be here long. I'm sorry for her. Well, what I'll do, I'll post a man outside the house nights from now on.

That'll cost the town three dollars a day. And ten dollars apiece to plant Shoup and Norton out of the taxpayers' pockets. Death and taxes, Books—what I just said. Keeping you alive long enough to die natural is costing us a pretty penny."

"I don't need a man outside."

"No? You may not, but I do. Things like last night make me look bad. Hell, there's already a crowd of loafers out front on Overland, gabbing and pointing. Maybe the Council could charge admission and get back a little." His wit pleased him. He elaborated. "We'll put up a sign—'See the Famous Killer, Ten Cents! Ten Cents More to See Him Draw!'"

"Not three minutes ago," commented Books, "you said in your profession you'd learned to keep your mouth shut."

The marshal stiffened, but his response to the slur on this visit was milder than it had been on the first. That had been a dress-up occasion; he had never before been face to face with a reasonable facsimile of J. B. Books; he had come prepared to lay down his life for the law if necessary. Now he condescended to an invalid, a man with one foot, one leg in fact, in the grave, and the other going, and he could afford to be at ease. He knew where the Remingtons were now, and he had every advantage of time and proximity. He rose, set his cup and saucer on the chiffonier, reseated himself, and crossed his legs.

"I'll speak my mind, Books. And I'll post a man starting tonight. We're not going to turn a decent woman's home into a shooting gallery. Shoup and Norton may be out of the way, but this town's full of hard cases who'd sell their souls to put your name on the wall. I'll see it don't happen."

Books was interested. "Who?"

"Jack Pulford for one. Runs the faro layout at Keating's."

"Gamblers. All bluff and no balls."

"Not this one. Straightest shot I've ever seen, and cool as a cucumber. Couple years back he got off one round here, under fire, through the heart, and they measured. Eighty-four feet. Through the heart."

"Who else?"

"Oh, a Mex name of Serrano. *El Tuerto*, they call him, 'Cross-eye.' He'll rustle a bunch of cattle over the river, sell 'em on this side, then rustle 'em back and sell 'em to the same outfit he rustled 'em from in the first place. A real cutthroat. I wouldn't turn my back on him in church."

"Who else?"

Thibido rubbed his chin. "Well, I've got a kid in my hoosegow now—Jay Cobb. His dad runs a creamery. Cobb's only twenty or so, but I'll hang him before he's thirty, or somebody will. Gun crazy—been toting one since he was big enough to lift it. I've got him in for thirty days on assault—broke a salesman's jaw with a butt. Oh, he's a wild kid. About like you were his age, I expect."

"Who else?"

"They'll do. Any of that three would prize to do you in. Any time you'd like to put 'em under, and clean up this town, yourself included, Council'll pay for the lead and four first-class wakes. How about it, Books? Do a good deed for once in your life."

Books examined a fingernail. "You'd miss us when we were gone, Thibido."

"Miss you? Sure, like the piles." He became grim. "I've already had run-ins with Serrano and Cobb. Pulford'll kill somebody else someday. They all need killing, and so do you." He pointed a finger. "You haven't looked at a calendar lately, Books. This is nineteen-ought-one. The old days are dead and gone and you don't even know it. You think this town's just another place to raise hell. Hell it is. Sure, we've still got the saloons and the girls and the tables, but we've also got a water-works and a gashouse and telephones and lights and an opera house, we'll have our streetcars elec-trified by next year, and there's talk about paving the streets. They killed the last rattler on El Paso Street two years ago, in a vacant lot. First National Bank's there now. We had the President of the United States in the plaza yesterday. Why, you can have ice delivered right to your door! Oh, we've still got some weeding to do, but once we're rid of the Pulfords and Cobbs and Serranos we'll have a goddam Garden of Eden here." The marshal's civic satisfaction was almost palpable. "Which leaves you, J. B. Books. Where do you fit into the prog-ress? You don't. You belong in a museum. To put it in a nutshell, Books, you've plain, plumb out-lived your time."

"A nutshell?" Books set his cup and saucer on the splintered library table. "You couldn't put it in a barrel with no bottom. You are the longest-winded bastard I ever listened to."

Thibido bristled. "Is that so? Well, I may be windy, but I'm not contrary! When my time comes to die I will, won't drag it out! Why the hell don't you?"

Books smiled. "I'm sticking around for your sake. When I am gone, how will you earn your pay? Checking door locks? Finding the lost cats for old ladies? You need me, Thibido. A man like me keeps you frisky. When I pull out, you'll go to grass."

"Horseshit!"

Books sobered. He was tired. He looked away, out a window, at the sunlight of another day. "You better mull one thing. When I die, part of you dies too. Maybe the best part."

Marshal Walter Thibido jumped to his feet. "I've heard about enough!" he rasped. "Kill two men before breakfast and scare the daylights out of law-abiding citizens—I won't take any Sunday school lessons from a low-life like you! Three dollars a night to guard a nickel-plate *pistolero* who's on his way anyway—you're not worth it, Books! Your whole rotten life hasn't been worth three cents!" Emboldened by his own oratory, he put a hand around the butt of his everyday Colt's. "Sympathy shit. What I should do is put you out of your misery," he threatened.

Deliberately, using both arms of the leather chair, Books pushed himself erect. As though there were no one else in the room, he stepped to the closet, pulled the curtain aside and leaned against the wall. He faced the marshal, one hand at idle rest on the jamb near which hung his coat and vest.

"You've worn out your welcome, Thibido," he said. "Now scat."

"Don't give me orders, Mr. Man-killer." The marshal removed his hand from his gun butt, however. 'I'll go when I'm ready. You'll go when you have to. Just do it soon. Get a move on. Die as damn fast as you can. It'll be a blessing."

"Want to see my specials again?" Books inquired.

Walter Thibido backed toward the door. "I don't scare any more, Books. Maybe you had me buffaloed the last time, but not now. Not in the shape you're in. So don't ride me. I don't scare."

"Neither did Shoup and Norton."

It had gone too far. Thibido knew it, but did not know how to extricate himself gracefully.

"You wouldn't gun down a peace officer," he claimed, without much assurance.

"Wouldn't I? What in hell would stop me? Fear of hanging?"

Bond Rogers sewed up the bullet holes in the mattress, remade the bed, and cleaned the mirror and washbowl. She did not speak to Books, nor he to her. Not until she was on her hands and knees, scrubbing dried blood out of the Wilton carpet under the south window, did he acknowledge her presence.

"Thibido says there's a crowd out in front of the house."

"There is."

He adjusted the crimson pillow under him. "I have to say I am sorry again. I assure you I am. Their names were Shoup and Norton. I have never heard of them in my life, or seen them before that I know of."

"But they're dead."

He raised his newspaper and pretended again to read. She continued to scrub. He lowered the paper. "Not long ago you told me I am a vicious, notorious individual utterly lacking in character or decency. If it will satisfy you, I will say amen to that. But I remind you. They came here to kill me. I did not have one damned thing against them."

She did not respond. He raised the paper, and after a minute lowered it again.

"I defended myself, that was all. As any man worth his salt would do."

"My roomers are gone," she said. "The first thing this morning. Now I have no income except from you. Thanks to you, I am dependent on a dying man, and his guns. I have already lost my son. Now there's every possibility I will lose my home."

He reflected. "We are both in a tight," he admitted. He frowned. "I will make it up to you, ma'am. I swear on stack of Bibles."

He waited, but she would not speak. When finished, she picked up her bucket and studied the carpet.

"Does the livery have a telephone?" he asked.

"I think so."

"Will you telephone them for me? Tarrant, that's his name. Tell him to come over here. I want to see him. Today."


"I am Books. How much of a bill have I run up at your establishment?"

Moses Tarrant could only stare.

"How much do I owe you?"

"Seven-fifty for the horse. So far."

"How much for the hire of the phaeton?"

"Ten dollars."

"Ten dollars!"

"Includes the team."

"It better. So, seventeen-fifty. All right, I want to sell the horse."

Moses Tarrant had a cold. With each breath he snuffled. From a pocket he drew a damp, dirty bandanna, unwadded it to locate an area as yet unused, located one, wrapped the bandanna about his nose, blew loudly, examined the area to see what he had blown, wadded the bandanna, and returned it to his pocket.

"Mr. Books, you joshing me?"

"I am not."

"You already sold that horse."

"The hell I have."

"You did so. This morning. Mrs. Rogers' boy, what's-his-name, come down and told me you wanted to sell. I gave him a hundred dollars for it."

Books hauled himself from his chair. "What in hell did you do that for? It isn't his horse, it's mine!"

"He told me! Just like he did about that phaeton! He told me you told him—"

"Tarrant, you have lost a hundred dollars."

His meaning did not immediately penetrate. When it did, a look of tragedy too real to be four-flush gripped Moses Tarrant's features. Perhaps he tried, in order to estimate the dimensions of his loss, to calculate how many nickel beers a hundred dollars would obtain. A fit of coughing overtook him. In dire straits he scanned the carpet and the corners of the room for a place to spit and finding none, took out his bandanna and employed it for the purpose.

"But he told me, that kid—"

"I don't give a damn what he told you. It's my animal, not his. Do you still want to buy it?"

"Reckon I might."

"I thought as much. I will have two hundred more for him."

"Two hunderd!" Tarrant hawked. "He's fistu-lowed!"

"Of course he is. And you should have him cured by now—you know how. Cauterize and the air will heal it. Otherwise he's in good condition."

"I might go a hundred."

Books glared at the liveryman. "You cheap snotnose. You know damn well you will sell him for a lot more because he belonged to John Bernard Books. Two hundred, and I will throw in my saddle. Cash."

"A hundred fifty?"

"Two hundred. Do you want to argue with me?"

"What about my bill?"

"You throw that in."

"That's three hundred seventeen-fifty! I ain't made of money!"

Books considered him. To avoid the consider-ation, the liveryman used his bandanna for lack of anything better to do. He snuffled; he blew. He coughed; he spat. But when done, when his respi-ratory problems had been temporarily solved, his pecuniary remained, and he was still the center of attention.

"Robbery" he insisted.

"So was stealing him from a kid for a hundred dollars."

Tarrant accepted the inevitable. Reaching into a pocket, he extracted a long leather snap-top purse which bulged, fished out a roll of bills and, wetting his thumb, peeled off two hundred dollars.

Books handled the bills with care, by the corners, and spread them on the library table to disinfect. "Now you take damned good care of that horse."

"Robbery."

"And on your way out, ask Mrs. Rogers and her son to come in here."

When they appeared after several minutes, Books stood behind the armchair, arms folded across his chest, his attitude controlled but temperish.

"Boy," he said without preamble, "you sold my horse to Tarrant this morning. You kept the money."

"Gillom!" his mother gasped. "You didn't!"

"Speak up," Books ordered.

"What if I did? How much'll you be riding from now on?"

"That's theft, or something kin to it. You got a hundred dollars for him. Where is it?"

Gillom chewed a sullen lip.

"I don't know what to say," Bond Rogers appealed. "Gillom, you make me ashamed of you. I can't—"

"Stay out of this," Books interrupted. "All right, son, produce that money or I will turn you upside down."

Gillom produced, and unfolded, two fifty-dollar bills.

"Give it to your mother."

"But it's yours," she protested to Books.

"It will pay for the bedding," he said. "And some of the inconvenience. Take it."

With a small bow and a smirk, Gillom placed it in her hand.

"Now I wish you'd leave us, ma'am. I want a few words with him."

It was an injunction. She started to say something about prerogative, then deferred to the male and left them, closing the door behind her.

"Now then, son," Books said. "You account to me."

"I told you. The name's Gillom."

"The name's 'thief' as I see it. And you'd better account to somebody."

"I don't have to. You got your money."

Books moved from behind the armchair. "You know, I started to take a liking to you. You are making it mighty hard for me, though. The more I learn about you, the less I approve. Catching you spying on me. Quitting school to smartaleck around Utah Street. And now this, selling my horse out from under me. As I understand it, you are a sorrow to your mother."

"So are you."

They were chin to chin. They were like two cottonwoods, but the ditch between them was deep, not shallow, and the water in it tainted.

"What did you plan on doing with the money?" Books asked.

"I planned to get the hell out of here."

"And do what?"

"Buy a gun and some fancy clothes. Kill a few barflies and get me a reputation."

"Don't get cute with me," Books warned.

"Don't you bullyrag me."

"If this house had a woodshed, we would do some business you wouldn't get over in a month of Sundays."

"Well, it don't. And you're not my father."

"No, thank God."

"Even if you would like to go to bed with my mother."

Books slapped him.

Gillom lunged, half in anger, half in fear, throwing one arm about the man's neck, the other about his waist. They grappled. And suddenly, to his amazement, almost to his dismay, the boy found his strength superior. They wrestled into the chiffonier. Gillom braced himself against it and, as the man seemed to give way, to collapse, with a shove threw him backward onto the bed.

J. B. Books lay on his back, breathing hard, shielding his face and his helplessness with a forearm. Gillom Rogers bent over him, triumphant.

"Haven't I learned a lot, though?" he gloated. "I'm as good with a gun as you. And you can't fight for sour apples, not any more you can't. So you just remember, Mister Blowhard—I've got my own laws now, just like you, and I live by 'em. I won't be laid a hand on either, or showed up. And I won't be treated like a kid, ever again."

Books groaned. "You sneaking little bastard."

Gillom laughed softly. "Hah. You dying old son of a bitch."


East of El Paso several miles the Rio Grande in its meanderings had divided, and by division formed between its halves an island. Consisting of some twenty acres of sand and brush, it was inhabited by snakes and insects, by bilingual cattle being rustled to and fro between Texas and Mexico, and by humans of two disreputable sorts: those commercially interested in the transit of the cattle and those preoccupied with their own transit between the jails of one country and the wide-open spaces of the other.

Six of the former indulged themselves this morning in a recreation known colloquially as "The Stretcher." Two were cowmen, older and wiser and more brutal than their employees, four cowboys. After relieving him of a pistol and a pair of knives, the six had thrown a seventh man to the ground, on his back, and, holding him down, had removed his shirt and boots. Above each of his wrists and ankles they tied a rope and, leading up four of their horses, attached the loose ends securely to the horns of the saddles. While the cowmen sat upon the victim, the cowboys mounted up and clucked the four horses slowly away from him, taking up slack. The lines went taut. The horses walked, step by step, until the victim's arms and legs were extended to the full. The two cowmen got off him. Another step, and another, by the obedient animals, and the struggling man was lifted from the ground, higher and higher, step by step. The horses were halted. The unfortunate captive now hung five feet above the ground, his joints stretched to the limit of physical tolerance by rope and the weight of the four ponies. Suppose now that the cowboys had slapped hats across the withers of the horses, causing them to catapult away. The ropes were stout enough to hold a steer. What must have occurred was the separation of arms and legs from sockets, then the ripping loose of limbs from the body—a literal dismemberment. But the cowboys dismounted instead and, sauntering back, grinning, joined their employers to squat and pass a bottle and to toast their skills.

The object of "The Stretcher" meanwhile hung suspended. He was a man in his late thirties, a man powerful and mustached, but also a man uniquely ugly. One cheek was scarred, and one brown eye, his left, was exotropic; it deviated outward, so that while his vision was in fact unimpaired he seemed to have the facility to attend two different things at once, in two different directions. This gave him an unnatural advantage, for it enabled him to concentrate simultaneously on criminal matters north and south of the border. He was noted for his achievements on both sides. North, it was said, he had murdered by knife; south, he had served time for the rape and strangulation, while drunk, of a girl nine years of age. He was sometimes referred to as *El Tuerto*, or "Cross-eye."

Presently he was engaged in conversation by the two cowmen. He had failed to deliver a certain number of head by a certain date—cattle neither his nor theirs. Worse yet, he had been advanced a sizable sum. Of this default the cowmen reminded him, and reminded him additionally that they had but to give the word, send the horses, and he would find himself, or various parts of himself, strewn over the valley from hell to breakfast.

The stretched man begged for his life. He was the sole support, he asserted, of a wife and ten small *niños*. His children would starve, his wife would take to the streets, and he called upon God and the Virgin and the generosity of the *Americanos* to spare him. He begged at the top of his voice. Sweat poured from his upper body. Blood welled from under the ropes above his wrists and ankles. The horses stood steady, disconcerting insects with their tails.

The cowboys laughed and passed the bottle. The two cowmen pondered El Tuerto's fate. One of them had a notion.

"Books is in El Paso. Some roomin' house. A goner, they say."

"I heard," said the other. "Killed two drifters tryin' to kill him."

"Serrano's s'pose' to be good with a gun."

"May be. Books is holed up, though. He won't come out."

"Shit he won't. He won't kick off in no bed. One of these days he'll come out for the bright lights and one more go-round. That's the time."

They pondered anew.

"Bear and a bulldog."

"You might be right."

"Want to try it?"

"Might's well. Might be fun."

They reclaimed the bottle and, standing, accompanied by the others, moseyed to the stretched man. His body quivered. A few minutes more under such skeletal tension and he would be on the brink of idiocy.

They made him a proposition. They had intended to kill him here, but they would give him a chance. Go into El Paso and wait for J. B. Books to come out of his hole. When he did, find him and draw on him.

El Tuerto babbled a disinclination.

They repeated the offer: agree to take Books on, or they would start the horses. If he killed Books, they would cancel his debt. If, on the other and more likely hand, Books killed him, everyone was square.

Serrano continued to demur.

One of the cowmen cupped a palm, poured from the bottle, and let a little whiskey into the rustler's exotropic eye. He screamed.

The cowmen smiled.

"If it doesn't sound too uppity, Mr. Books, I am the premier photographer hereabouts," said Mr. Skelly. "I have photographed the most prominent citizens of El Paso—male and female. And I'd be pleased—and honored—to do a full-length portrait of you—on the best solio paper. Free of charge."

"Why?"

"Why, why because you're a famous man, sir. Next to Mr. McKinley—I photographed him, by the way—one of the most famous visitors to our fair city in years. It will give my studio—what shall I say?—style. Normally charge four dollars a dozen for portraits. You shall have a dozen with my compliments."

Books considered him.

"You can send them to friends and relatives—a treasured keepsake."

Mr. Skelly prided himself on his salesmanship.

"That's the time a man should be photographed, sir—when he's in his prime—the full bloom of his manhood. Too often we let things slide until it's too—"

"All right," Books consented.

Skelly clapped his hands. "Fine! Fine! Now if you'll just slip into a coat, please, I'll bring in my camera and equipment. Right on the front porch—won't be a minute, sir!"

When the photographer returned, Books waited by the bed in vest and Prince Albert coat. Skelly put down his case and stood the camera on his tripod.

"The latest, most modern equipment, I assure you, Mr. Books. A Conley eight-by-ten camera with a twelve-inch rectilinear lens—the best money can buy. Now let me see."

He surveyed the room and settled on the open area between the chiffonier and the south window, posing his subject against the wall of lilies. He then stationed his camera, turned the base cogwheel to raise the red maplewood box to the proper height, and turned a second cogwheel to run out the bellows. His focusing cloth was cut from the green baize of a billiard table top. Draping it over the box and his head and shoulders, he stooped to the ground glass and adjusted his bellows to correct focus.

"There. There. I have you now, Mr. Books."

From his case he took a plateholder and inserted it in the camera, then brought out a variety of objects—a tin trough, a wooden handle, a small bottle of alcohol with a wick in the top, a length of quarter-inch brass pipe, and a box of magnesium powder. Affixing the wooden handle beneath the trough, he poured into it a mustard spoonful of powder, set the bottle of alcohol in its holder behind the trough, and attached the length of pipe so that one end opened near the bottle wick.

"What in hell is that thingumajig?" Books inquired.

"Why, my flashpan, sir—a recent invention. There's never light enough indooors—so we make our own. Now one more thing—this powder pops very bright and very slow—a one-twenty-fifth-of-a-second flash. Startles the dickens out of some of my customers—they'll flinch or blink and ruin the whole thing. Are you sure you'll hold still when she goes? When you're under fire? A photographer's joke."

"I am sure."

"If you aren't, I have a headholder outside. Stand it up behind you out of sight—clamps your head like a vise."

"I said I am sure."

"Fine. Now one last thing, Mr. Books. Stand erect, please. And if you won't take offense—please put your hands in your trouser pockets—to draw back the lapels of your coat."

"Why?"

"Well, sir, they tell me you carry your weapons in a most unusual manner. If we could catch just a glimpse—just a glimpse, mind you—of the handles, it would add—what shall I say?—a certain style to the portrait."

Books scowled but shoved his hands in his pockets, squared his shoulders, and Skelly ducked once more under his focusing cloth.

"There they are! Perfect, sir! Now, by George!"

He folded the green cloth, tucked it away in his case, pulled the side from the plateholder, and striking a match on the seat of his pants, lit the wick atop the bottle. In his left hand he grasped the squeeze bulb, in his right the flashpan, tilting it at a forty-five-degree angle.

"Ready, Mr. Books? Assume whatever expression you think appropriate, sir—something on the— what shall we say?—threatening side, perhaps. Don't move now—this is for American history!"

Skelly stuck one end of the brass pipe in his mouth and squeezed the bulb and puffed into the pipe and his exhalation blew the alcohol flame through a hole at the rear of the tin trough and ignited the magnesium powder and for one twenty-fifth of a second, while the shutter opened, the room was lit celestially. Instantly thereafter it was darkened by a pall of acrid smoke, and by the time Books had blinked, Skelly had put down the flashpan, extinguished the flame, whisked two cardboard squares from his case, flung up the windows, and was fanning smoke as his subject hacked and coughed and further profaned the atmosphere with curses.

"Sorry, sir! A small price to pay—for the photographic art!"

Beaming, eyes shut, he fanned with might and main till visibility was restored. When it was, gratification vanished from his countenance in much less than one twenty-fifth of a second. Books's face was close to his, and the expression on the gun man's face was, whether appropriate or not, unmistakably threatening.

"You are giving me a dozen pictures, is that right, Skelly?"

"Yes, sir," Skelly swallowed.

"All I need is one."

"Yes, sir."

"How many more can you make?"

"From the negative? Why, as many as I care to—I guess."

"And you will care to make one hell of a number, won't you?"

"Why, why should I, Mr. Books?"

"Because I am dying and you know God damned well I am, don't you?"

"I—I heard something of that—what shall I say? —nature, sir. I regret—"

"And you will turn out pictures of the famous mankiller like sausages, won't you? And peddle 'em for a dollar a crack, won't you?"

"Oh, Mr. Books—how could you think—a man in my position—"

"So here's what you do, Skelly. You send me over my one as damn soon as you can, and fifty dollars cash with it. Or I will come down to your place of business and ram some of that powder up your rear end and put the end of a cigar to it and there will be a hot time in your ass that night. Do you follow me, you cheapskate?"

"Yes, sir!"

Jan. 22: Peter Donley, an old-time Arizonan, killed himself with a revolver at Briggs in Yavapai County. He asked a man who was stopping with him to go and get him some whiskey. While he was gone Donley placed a Colt's revolver in his mouth and pulled the trigger. The bullet was a big one and broke his jawbone and neck. It is supposed that he killed himself because he was suffering with the grippe.

He stopped reading to take laudanum. He resorted to it every two hours now, night and day, and had used half the twelve-ounce bottle.

Before picking up the paper he listened to the high ringing sound, iron on iron, like that of clapper on bell, as the nine o'clock streetcar passed the corner on its last run.

He was bone lonesome. Once, years ago, up in the Dakotas, he and three others had staked out a claim, and while his partners had gone off to Deadwood to register it and obtain tools and provisions, he had lived alone on the claim. For two weeks he roughed it in the rain, under a black sky. Later, he had had to kill one of his partners to get his share of the dust, a middling amount but rightfully his. But here, tonight, with a roof over his head, reading by an electric light and listening to a streetcar, people sleeping above him, in the heart of a city, he was lonesomer than he had been up in the Dakotas in the rain, under a black sky.

Jan. 22: An Albuquerque dispatch says: Francis Schlader, the "Healer," who is attracting so much attention in the Territory and elsewhere because of his marvelous power to heal the sick and cause the blind to see, yesterday calmly and bluntly announced that he is Christ. Among his callers night before last was Rev. Charles L. Bovard. Rev. Bovard tells of the interview in the following letter:

"My object was to settle from his own statements just what he claims to be and do. It seemed to me that the Christian people and sensible people in general ought to know what he avows. After several questions of less import, I asked him plainly: 'Do you claim to be Jesus Christ returned to earth?' Looking me steadily in the eye with a demoniac glare, he answered: 'I am. Since you have asked me, sir, I say plainly, I am!' I did not argue with him. Life is too short to waste time trying to teach a jackass to sing soprano."

He slept soundly, but only for an hour. Discomfort waked him then, and though he dozed, on and off, resisting the succor of the drug, in half an hour he could endure the torment no longer. He sat up in bed, and in the dark reached for the bottle with such clumsy desperation that he knocked the glass candy compote off the table to the floor. He swore and, fumbling, found the bottle and put his mouth to the top like a child to the breast.

He thought: For babies and grown men: Ol' Doc Hostetler's El Paso Paregoric.

He had to sit now. The effect of the laudanum was not only of shorter duration but each dose took longer to bring him surcease. He got out the chamber pot and tried for several minutes to use it, but in vain. His bladder was distended; it hung in his guts like a great rock. "You will gradually become uremic," the physician had said when pressed. "Poisoned by your own waste, due to a failure of the kidneys."

He thought: The hell I will. I will stay up as long as I have to. Piss or bust.

After a time the quaking tendons of his calves and thighs would not support him. By means of the bed he hauled himself to his feet, despairing. Any dog could lift a leg. This was what he had come to. A shell of a man squatting over a slop-jar in the dark, praying not for happiness or fame or nerve or fortune but the simple animal ability to unload.

He went to an open window and let himself down on his knees before it. It was snowing. He put out his hands and was pleased by the melt of flakes upon his flesh. Somewhere, out in the night close by, earning his three dollars, a man guarded him, some poor bastard who would rather be home in bed than watch over the life of one who was soon to lose it. He heard a mockingbird, astonished by the snow, singing in a tree. Its song was lovely. For some reason it reminded him of the four lines of poetry Hostetler had recited for him, but he could recall only the first: "Weave a circle round him thrice . . ." Two other lines were all the poetry he knew: "Under the spreading chestnut tree/the village smithy stands. . . ."

He thought: When we were kids, we used to play a game. "I Wish." Well, I wish I had listened to birds more often.

I wish I had more schooling.

I have strayed the western parts of the U. S., it must be the most beautiful country God ever made, and I wish I had paid more attention to it.

If wishes were horses, beggars would ride—but I have sold my horse.

I wish the last man I killed, in Tonopah, up in Nevada, had killed me.

I wish I had not been so good with guns so early.

I wish I had been born peaceable.

My strength is gone. That was one of the most shameful things I ever remember, being flat on my back with a string-bean kid laughing at me.

It won't be long now. A month? Three weeks? Two? Jesus.

I wish I had married Serepta, and settled down, and had a son to leave my guns to. I was forty then, and she was twenty-eight.

I wish I had been to San Francisco.

Hostetler said one morning I will wake up and know I can't get out of bed. I have to beat that morning by one. So it is a matter of timing, as it usually is. If I am going to make a move, I must do so before it is too late, even twenty-four hours too late. But first I have to decide the move.

I wish I had sailed on a ship just once, and seen the Sandwich Isles.

I wish I had not left home so young. I would like to know what became of my people.

Bond. A crackerjack name for a woman. She is sorry for me, but she wants me dead and I do not blame her. I was wrong about her. She has class. But she also has plenty of starch in her corset. She speaks up to me. She will scrub blood out of a carpet. She may be a lady on the outside, but inside she is full of the Old Harry, and I have not met many like that. I could love her. Given time, I could make her love me, but that would not be fair. Given time, I could straighten out that boy. Somebody had better do it soon, or he will go the way I did, or worse. Given time. I wish I knew why he hates me. Not three days ago he thought I was ace high. Given time.

I wish I had not been such a loner all my life.

I wish I had been more worthy of love, and given a damn sight more.

God I wish I had it to do all over again. I would do it better.

He left the window and tried the pot again, this time with a dribble of success, then got back into bed and touched each Remington to be certain it was where it should be.

He thought: Shoup and Norton were names I really did not know, but there are three I will remember: Jack Pulford; Serrano; Jay Cobb. They would sell their souls, Thibido said, to put my name on the wall.

So. I had no show to win before. Now I have. It is a game of draw poker now. I am the dealer now, not a God damned cancer. Not death. I can call the play. I can hold my pair, my guns, and draw three cards:

One. I can lie here and die slow.

Two. Or I can blow out my own brains. But I have too much sand for that. Besides, it has no style. There would be no honor in it. It is not the way that J. B. Books should go.

Three. The third card. Or I can pick my own executioner.

I wish I knew which one of them is the sure shot. I wish I knew which one deserves to kill me.

What was that line? Yes. "Weave a circle round him thrice . . ."

Pulford.

Serrano.

Cobb.

# Four

"There's a man to see you," she announced. "A Mr. Beckum."

Books was lathering his face. "See me about what?"

"I intended to tell you who he is. I'm well acquainted with your temper. I can still see that poor young reporter flying down the front steps."

"Well?"

"He's an undertaker."

Books put down his brush and mug to turn and look at her.

"We have three in town. He's the best known. I must say he's being a little forward. Of course, you don't have to see him."

He went back to his lather, scowling into the mirror. "It snowed last night," he said.

"Yes. It's melted this morning, though." She could almost hear him thinking.

"Thibido said he was putting a man outside the house at night. Did he?"

"Yes. He strolls up and down across Overland. Most of the time he leans against a tree. I'm not sure how effective it is."

"If it bothers you, I can tell Thibido to take him off."

"No. I don't mind."

He finished lathering. "All right. Send him in."

She hesitated.

"Don't' worry, we'll get along. He's probably come by to thank me."

"Thank you?"

His smile was foamy and sardonic. "On behalf of his profession."

When his visitor entered, Books was stropping a razor suggestively on the palm of his hand. "Come in. Have a seat."

"Thank you." Uncertain of his reception, however, and immediately aware of the razor, Beckum remained standing. "I hope you don't mind my stopping by, Mr. Books. That is I hope you don't think it untimely."

"Not at all. I like to see a businessman with get-up-and-go."

Despite the black he wore, Beckum was the picture of rotund, hog-jowled health. He was practiced in two attitudes: a heartiness which belied the imminence of death and a gravity underlined the transience of life. He alternated them like pairs of shoes, getting the most wear out of both.

"I admit to hearing certain—certain unfortunate things about your physical condition, Mr. Books," he said gravely. "I came by to express my heartfelt regret."

Books began to shave. "And?"

"And to discuss something with you. As you know, there are certain—certain arrangements which must be made, and practical folks often make them in advance. That is, we are mortal men, Mr. Books, all of us, and if we are prudent as well, we—"

"What's your proposition?"

"A simple business one, sir. You are a very respected and prominent individual," said the undertaker heartily. "Seeing to the final details for you would attest to the excellence of my mortuary service. To be truthful, the kind of advertising money can't buy. Therefore I am prepared to offer you embalming by the most scientific methods, a bronze coffin guaranteed good for a century regardless of climatic or geological conditions, my best hearse, the minister of your choice, the presence of at least two mourners, a headstone of the finest Carrara marble, a plot of a size and in a location befitting your status, and perpetual care of the grounds."

"For how much?"

"For nothing, sir. For the privilege."

"How much will you clear on the deal?"

"I beg your pardon. You must be joking. I'll be out a very large sum, I assure—"

"In a pig's ass you will."

"I misunderstand you, sir."

Razor arrested, Books paused to consider the reflection in the mirror of the undertaker behind him, who seemed in turn to be mesmerized by the reflection, half lather, half menace, of the gun man before him.

"Here's what you will do, Beckum. Just what did they do to Hardin here, after he was gone. I read about it. You will lay me out and let the public in to have a look at fifty cents a head, children ten cents. Then when the curiosity peters out you will pick the gold out of my teeth and wrap me in a gunny sack and stick me in a hole somewhere and hustle your loot to the bank."

"Mr. Books, I assure you—"

"Assure me? What the hell good will your word be when my veins are full of your God damned juice? Who will keep you to it?"

The undertaker shuffled his feet, confused as to which pair of shoes he should be wearing.

Books raised his blade, resumed shaving. "No, here's what you will do, Beckum. I want your guarantee I will have a proper grave. Later. And I want a cut of the proceeds and a headstone. Now. Cash in hand and a stone to be delivered in two days or sooner. I want a small stone, good quality, with this on it—'John Bernard Books 1849-1901.' That's all. No angels or jabbery. Got that?"

"I find such an arrangement distasteful, sir. That is—"

"Or I will go to your competitors and deal with them."

"I see. You're a hard man, Mr. Books."

"Not hard. Alive. And the living drive harder bargains than the dead." Books rinsed his face and dried it with a towel. "I'll have fifty dollars now."

Beckum pinched the tip of his nose. "That's too high. If I deliver a stone and give you fifty, I'm cutting it too thin. I've done some arithmetic, and my guess is no more than three hundred will want to view the remains."

"Three hundred? You underestimate me."

"Shoup and Norton have been a great help, I must say. If you could manage to shoot—"

"I'll see what I can do."

"Thirty's my top, sir."

"Forty. Run an ad in the paper."

Beckum sighed and reached for his wallet. "Very well, forty it is." He handed Books two twenties. "I'll set my stonecutter to work on the inscription at once."

"Two days or sooner," Book repeated. "I am running out of time."

The undertaker put away his wallet and shook a solemn head. "I am grieved to hear it, Mr. Books. I am deeply grieved."

He knew the comings and goings of the house as well by now as the comings and goings of his pain. The boy was out for the evening. He could hear the mother running water in the bathroom down the hall. He gave himself a whore's bath at the washbowl daily, but he would need a real one soon, in a tub, and doubted he could do it by himself.

The salaries paid to the Prince of Wales out of the British treasury add up to $680,000 a year, and he has a private income besides. Nevertheless Andrew Carnegie, the laird of Skibo castle, could buy him out several times over and still have enough left to give away a library or two when he felt like it.

That reminded him. Taking his time, he pulled himself out of the armchair and, working slowly along the brass rail at the foot of the bed, reached the chiffonier, opened the top drawer, and counted his money. There was two hundred dollars from the sale of his horse, and Beckum's forty. And the photographer, Skelly, owed him a portrait and another fifty, plus what he had in his wallet. At this rate he would soon be another Andrew Carnegie.

He closed the drawer, worked his way back to the chair, and taking up the newspaper again, read two filler items:

Rumors that Professor Garner, the monkey talk man, was dangerously ill and in distress in Africa have been denied. He is pursuing his studies in Simian conversation as enthusiastically as ever, and is enduring the deprivations and dangers of life in a savage country with the hope of gleaning from the chatter of the apes some slight addition to the facts of science.

Bishop Potter's proposal to organize a vigilance committee of five thousand to inquire into the causes of New York's rottenness is causing Tammany to tremble in its shoes. Poor old Tammany is having a hard time to bluff through these days.

He was ten years old and riding in a spring wagon behind a team of mules with his grandfather, who was driven occasionally to desperate undertakings. They were making a journey of forty miles and two days across San Saba County to the farm of relatives, cousins. His grandmother had three months previously gone to visit the cousins, and while there had died of a fever and been buried. For the three months of his bereavement his grandfather had brooded. It was not right that his wife should lie in alien soil; he wanted her home again, near him, on the home place. He could not eat, would not rest; he talked to himself. And so, finally, old man and boy set out upon their journey. When they reached the cousins, they dug up the coffin, a plain box of gumwood, and hoisting it into the wagon, started homeward. The sun was hot, the way endless. On the first day the lid and sides of the coffin began to swell. By midmorning of the second day the bloating of the corpse had attained such proportions that nails and gumwood could not contain it. The lid burst open. A great groan escaped, and stench. They stopped the team and hammered at the lid, in the heat and stench they jumped up and down on it, they danced upon it, ki-yi-ing like crazed Comanches, desperate grandfather and terrified grandson, until they were exhausted, until they vomited, but to no avail. They drove on and, detouring to a village, applied to the blacksmith for help. The smith a mighty man was he, and the coffin was soon sealed tight with iron bands. They took it home then, and reburied her in the shade of a live-oak tree, and put up a simple wooden cross, and his grandfather, whose name was Galen Books, would sit by the grave in the evenings, and chew tobacco, and explain to his wife what they had done, and why.

He burst from dreams and covers, groaning, to sit bolt upright in bed. His longjohns were damp with sweat, but in a moment he was cold, and shivered. He groped for the bottle but could not find it.

With an oath he pulled the lamp chain, blinked in the light, and drinking from the bottle, grimacing at the bitterness, capped it. He looked at his

watch, a good gold Elgin with a small diamond centered in the case cover. It was not quite two o'clock
in the morning. The last dose had enabled him to
sleep for less than an hour.

But this one did not relieve him. Pain grew into
agony. The disease was ravaging him now, feeding
on its cell to create new cells, extending itself
throughout the lower third of his trunk. Pins, nee-
dles, scissors, knives stabbed him, were withdrawn,
and stabbed again and again. He let himself slide
from the bed to the floor and placed his forearms
on the arms of the leather chair and rocked his
pelvis back and forth as though he were a child
riding a hobbyhorse. He yearned to cry out, to
wake the house, the town, the world, to the enormity of his suffering.

"Oh Jesus," he whimpered. "Sweet Jesus. What
have I done to deserve this? Oh, I can't go on
much longer. Jesus, Jesus, Jesus Christ."

The laudanum failed him. Staggering, he stumbled to the closet, swept the curtain aside, found
the whiskey on the shelf, uncorked, and poured it
down. He put the bottle back and waited, trembling,
to be eased.

Suddenly his stomach convulsed. Reeling forward, falling to his knees, he jerked out the slop-
jar and vomited, ridding himself not only of the
remnants of his supper but the laudanum—he realized too late—as well. And then, emptied, on
hands and knees, head hanging over his own spew,
teeth chattering with cold, in that animal posture
he knew fear for the first time in his adult life.

"Oh God," he whispered. "Oh my God I am
afraid to die."

He closed his eyes in fear. Out of nowhere the

second line came to him, and in his mind he added it to the first: "Weave a circle round him thrice/ And close your eyes with holy dread . . ."

He opened them. On the frosted lampshade by the bed, blue, brown, and green birds of paradise seemed to flap contemptuous wings at him.

Fear convulsed to rage. Rage endowed him with a strength he had not felt for days. Erupting up, he snatched the glass compote from the table and hurled it wildly, shattering it against the wall of lilies.

He was unappeased. Lurching to the closet, he tore one of the Remingtons from its holster and, hanging onto the curtain rod, threatened the ceiling with the weapon.

He thought: God! You hear me, God? Maybe I don't believe in you, but you damned well better believe in me! J. B. Books! See this gun? I kill with it! You kill, too, but I make a slicker job of it. I kill bad men, you kill good. I have reason, you don't. You are killing me hellish slow, and I do not deserve such treatment. You wrong me, and I will not be wronged. So let us have it out, God. Face me! Be a man and face me now if you have the guts—stand and draw or back off! God damn you, God, throw down on me and kill me now or let me live!

She did not know him.

He did not know her.

To surprise him, she had entered without knocking. He sat in shirt sleeves in a leather armchair on crimson pillow trimmed with golden tassels.

They haunted each other.

"Johnny?"

"Ma'am?"

She came closer.

"Johnny, don't you know me?"

Suddenly he did. It was her voice. Only her voice was the same.

"Serepta!"

"Yes! Yes!"

She ran to him. He did not rise but lifted both arms and spread them to receive her, and she stopped beside him while he took her in his arms and pulled her close and pressed his face to her hair and they laughed together, softly, and murmured to each other until he held her away so that he could look at her again. There were tears in his eyes.

"My God, I'm glad to have you here, Ser! I thought nobody I ever knew would come see me!"

"Oh, Johnny dear!" She leaned to kiss him on the mouth. "I came as soon as I heard!"

"Here. Sit up here, on the bed, near me."

He helped her. They smiled at each other, and she dabbed at her eyes with a handkerchief. "Have I changed so much, Johnny?"

"No. You have not. It has been so damned long, that's all."

"Eleven years."

But he had lied to her, gallantly. She was blowsy now, a blowsy, irrevocable thirty-nine. Her face was puffed and lined, and she had slathered on the rouge and powder and plucked her eyebrows into brazen arches. When she removed her bonnet the auburn mane he remembered had been clipped inexpertly to a shag, and rinsed with henna. He was sure he could not have changed as radically. Love had been her life eleven years ago, to give and to take. La, la, la, she had sung beneath him, a song as lovely as that of a mockingbird enraptured by snow. Now her concerns were probably spider webs at the corners of her eyes, a touch of arthritis on a rainy day, perhaps a bunion. His heart reconciled him to this new, this old Serepta Thomas, however, and to the treachery the years had done her. She was here, that was what counted, when he needed her, and he was grateful. He would take today with him to the grave.

"It isn't true, is it? About you?"

"That I have a cancer?"

"Yes."

"God how I loved you, Ser."

"And I loved you. It isn't true."

"It is."

"How long do they give you?"

"Weeks."

"Oh Johnny, no." She turned her head and used her handkerchief again.

"Don't cry, Ser. We all have our time. How did you know?"

"You're famous, and bad news travels fast. I'm living in Tucson now, and the day I heard I got right on the train."

"Good girl."

He took her handkerchief and brushed beneath her eyes. The cloth was frayed, and smelled of fivepenny perfume.

"I must look a sight."

"For sore eyes," he smiled. "Why did you come?"

"Why do you think? To see you again, to be with you. I haven't forgotten, Johnny. I never will."

He took her hands in his. They were chapped. He had lived with her in Tularosa for two years.

She had not asked marriage, nor had he offered it, because he was with her one day, gone the next. Then, when he returned one time from Colorado, she had left him for a freighter named Pardee.

"Are you still with Pardee?"

"No. He took off for California last year. Just up and skipped."

"Leaving me for a freighter. There was no future in that. Didn't you know the railroads were coming?"

"Oh, he made good money at first, and he was decent to me. He never carried a gun. Then there was less and less to haul and he started drinking. After that it was the old sad story—I had the same black eye for six months. When it would go to clear up, he'd freshen it."

"Did you have kids?"

"Two. Two girls."

"I'd have given you boys, Ser."

"And a black veil too. I couldn't have stood it, Johnny, watching you go off and worrying were you coming back alive or dead."

"Look how long I lasted."

She shook her head. "I couldn't have stood it. I loved you too much."

"We should have married."

"Spilt milk."

"We should have."

"You never did?"

"No."

"And you're alone. That's just awful. I'm so glad I came."

"So am I." He put her hands to his lips. "Oh God I am."

"Would you still like to?" she asked.

"What?"

"Get married."

"Now?"

"That's something I wanted to talk to you about. Life's bunged me up pretty bad, Johnny. I'm not near forty yet, and no prospects. I had to scrape to buy a train ticket. We could just call a minister and say 'I do.' I'd have the certificate. I'd have something to go on."

His smile was wry. "Not much. I've sold my horse. I have two guns and a gold watch."

"I'd have your name."

"How far would that take you?"

"A long ways, maybe."

He freed her hands. "How?"

"You're too modest, Johnny. You don't know what a high mogul you are. Shoot, everybody's heard of J. B. Books—everybody talks about you. You're in the papers all the time. And after you're gone, I'd be Mrs. J. B. Books, your widow. I'd be somebody."

"That wouldn't buy you bacon."

"Well, it might." She moistened her lips with the tip of her tongue. "You see, that's how I heard you were ailing bad. There's a newspaper reporter here in El Paso. He tracked me down someways and wrote me to come see him. So I did, this morning, on my way here. He wants to get out a book on you—you know, your life and killings and such—he'd write it and put my name on it—*The Shootist: The Life and Bloody Times of J. B. Books,* by Serepta Books. His Wife—he says it would sell back East like a house afire. He'd split it with me."

He lay back in his chair, away from her. "His name Dobkins?"

"Yes. How'd you know?"

"I kicked him out of here the other day."

"Why?"

"He wanted to do the same thing with me, only in the newspapers. The yellow-shoe son of a bitch. He's a sticker, though. He won't quit."

They were silent. She was gauging him. After a moment she put on a pout.

"I never did understand you, Johnny," she pouted. "I still don't. What's the harm in it? A wedding certificate—a piece of paper."

"I don't object to that. The book I do."

"Why?"

"How much do you know about my life? How much does Dobkins know?"

"Well, two years I do—what a lover you were. And what all you told me. He said whatever we don't know he'll make up. You know, gory things— shot-'em-ups and midnight rides and women tearing their hair!" She laughed. "Oh, it'll be a corker, Johnny, I promise!"

His look shut her like a door.

"No," he said. "I will not be remembered for a pack of lies."

She had been sure of him, of the natural advantage of the well over the ill. Now she did not know what way to go, whether to try for his soft side or to indict him for a hard heart. She tossed an emotional coin.

"It cost me three dollars for the train here, Johnny," she said, knotting her handkerchief. "One way."

"I'll buy you a ticket back."

"I gave you two years of my life. Can't you help me now, when I need it? My little girls—"

"Yours and Pardee's, not mine."

"But what's so wrong about a book?"

"I may not have much else, woman, but I still have my pride."

"Shit!" She let her anger go. "Pride. You've done enough harm to others in your life—can't you do a good deed for once?"

"So that's why you came to see me."

"I came because I need help!" she cried. "And you could give it and you won't, you're too damn mule-mean, you always were! Why should you care anyway—you're dying! I have to go on living—but you don't give a damn what becomes of me! Why should you? You won't be here!"

She had gone too far. He was considering her. And though eleven years had passed, she remembered: against that silent, terrible appraisal of his, nothing prevailed, neither tears nor accusation nor a bullet. She was frightened. She flung herself from the bed to the floor, she knelt between his legs, she tried to reclaim him with her arms.

"Oh, Johnny, shame on me! I shouldn't have said that! It's just I'm in such bad straits and so alone!"

She had an inspiration. "Johnny dear, I still love you, honest I do! I'd do anything for you!" She pulled his face forward, close to hers, and kissed him on the forehead, on the cheeks. She kissed him on the mouth, moaning passionately, forcing her tongue between his teeth. "Sweetie, there is something I can do for you." With one hand she reached between his legs and began to unbutton his fly. "Are you equal to it, Johnny?"

He groaned. His eyes were closed. Confidence returned, she thrust her hand inside his trousers, though the slit of his underwear, searching for his member. "Where's my gun? Will it still shoot, you old stallion? Wouldn't you like one last lay? Oh, dearie, I would!"

He fell back in his chair. "Go ahead, Ser—see what you find."

"Find? What?"

"The cancer!" he rasped. "That's where it is! If that's what you want, you whore, I'm full of it!"

"Ohhh!" Revolted, she snatched her hand away, she pushed herself from him, sprawling against the bed, sickened. She got to her feet and backed from him, her face a painted mask of loathing.

"You bastard," she spat.

In impotence, in utter despair, he covered his face with his hands. "My God," he said. "That's all you came for. And once I loved you. God help me."

"You killer."

"Good-by, Ser."

"May you rot to death," she hissed.

"In the closet, my wallet," he said hopelessly, his voice almost inaudible. "Take your three dollars. And good-by."

Marshal Thibido let him out of his cell in the city jail at exactly ten o'clock on Tuesday night. He could have been freed that afternoon, for it was the final day of his sentence for assault, but Thibido was adamant: the wet-ear son of a bitch would serve a full thirty days to the minute.

In the office, he gave him back his two Colt's revolvers and double holster and Cobb belted them on, tying each holster down midway of the thigh with a leather thong.

"Thanks for nothin', Marshal."

"You're not welcome. And they're not loaded. If you want to buy ammunition, you'll have to go work for your dad again. Your credit's no good and nobody else in his right mind would hire you." Thibido paused. "If you want my advice, don't buy any. Head for that wagon instead of a saloon. If you don't, if you go on the way you have been, I will hang you one of these days or somebody by God will."

"Thanks for nothin', Marshal."

Jay Cobb drew the revolvers and extended them, handles forward, as though to surrender them to Thibido. Suddenly, by means of index fingers through the triggerguards, he twirled the weapons, reversing them so that the muzzles pointed at the marshal's waistline.

He grinned. "That there's the Curly Bill Spin, Marshal. Ain't many can do it."

Thibido had recoiled at the trick. He caught relish on the faces of the two deputies who lounged against the wall, enjoying the show. To control himself, he took a deep breath.

"Cobb," he said, "you're no Brocius. He was a good criminal, the real cheese. You're a pimple-faced, short-pudded, yellow-assed kid, and you'll never grow up to be a good criminal because you don't have the brains to."

"These was loaded," Cobb blustered, "you wouldn't mouth me like that."

Thibido nailed hands to hips. "You're contaminating my premises. Take those popguns and your ugly self out of here or I'll telephone J. B. Books and sic him on you."

Jay Cobb did not know how to respond. His mouth opened and closed. He was twenty and ugly. His face had been scarred by acne, and there were swellings on each side of his neck, pustules, some of them open and inflamed. To compensate, he had taken early to guns. He practiced handling and marksmanship regularly down by the river, fanning his Colt's and cutting sunflower stalks in two. Gillom Rogers had spied out his pastime, and in return for secrecy Cobb had let him fire the weapons. Sunflowers grew wild and high in a large patch there—the very patch in which George Scarborough had killed Martin Morose while Morose was on his way from Juárez to confront John Wesley Hardin, who was living with Morose's wife in El Paso. Cobb knew that. He liked learning to use his guns with death nearby for a teacher.

"Old Books," he sneered. "He's dyin'. You call 'im and tell 'im to come see me. I'll hurry his dyin' along."

"So you broke some dude drummer's jaw," said one of the deputies. "You faced anybody, killed anybody?"

Cobb's mouth opened and closed.

"Go home before I puke," Thibido said.

Cobb's mouth opened and closed. He looked as though he wanted to kill someone or cry.

"Go home and wash your face," said a deputy.

Jay Cobb did go home, but not to the house beside the creamery. Entering the creamery by a back door and skulking between the separators and churns and stacked milk cans to the sales counter in front, he first reloaded his guns from a Bull Durham bag of ammunition he kept hidden in a drawer. He then opened the tin box in which his father stored the cash receipts before banking them on Fridays. Since quitting school, Jay had driven the delivery wagon and would be expected by his parents, who were meek, scriptural people, to take the route again now that he had been released from jail. Emptying the box of its contents, less than a hundred dollars, he left the building and the odors of milk and cream and butter, as far as he was concerned, forever.

He went directly to Tillie Howard's parlor house on Utah Street, by consensus the most lavish sexorium in town, its girls the most beautiful and expensive. The house was new, made of yellow brick with dormer windows and balconies before the windows on the second story, a circular drive, and a carriage house. He was admitted to the living room, a grand salon of crimson velvet draperies, silk and satin upholstery, oil paintings in gilt frames, cut flowers, and Aubusson rugs. There were few patrons this Tuesday night. Young Cobb whiled away a pleasant hour in the salon, pigging good whiskey and being edified by the staff until he made his selection. Choosing a blond enchantress in her late twenties named Vickie, and a full bottle, he escorted her upstairs to her room and locked the door. He was quite drunk by this time. And he had never kissed a member of the opposite sex other than his mother, much less known one carnally.

After both disrobed, he took Vickie and bottle to bed, but such was his state of inebriation that he was unable to consummate his desire. Blaming her for his impotence, Cobb flew off the handle. In a demented fury, taking out on the unfortunate girl a marginal intelligence, a repellent exterior, an adolescence spent upon the seat of a creamery wagon, thirty days in jail, and his treatment by the marshal and deputies, he pried open her legs and attempted to rape her with the barrel of one of his

Colt's. He tore her labia with the sight. She bled. She screamed. He beat her savagely with his fists.

Summoned by her appeals, the girls flew up the stairs in the wake of Jim, the general factotum of the house, a giant Negro who wore full dress in the evenings. He was nick-named "Gentleman Jim" after James Corbett, the heavyweight boxing champion only recently deposed by "Fighting Bob" Fitzsimmons. Jim battered down the door of the room and, obtaining Jay Cobb by the neck, dragged him downstairs and hurled him out the door.

He lay naked on the graveled drive while Vickie was ministered to by her colleagues. Presently they gathered in a bevy on a balcony and threw down to him, at him, in addition to expletives of a gender more masculine than feminine, his belongings—underwear, boots, shirt, hat, and eventually his guns. One of these hit him. He came to. Groveling for a revolver, he commenced firing at the balcony. Jay Cobb failed to kill any of the girls, who took refuge behind the balusters, or even to wound one, but he would have if he could have.

"You seem in fine fettle today," she said.

It was the first time she had seen him on the bed during the day.

"I should be," he smiled. He was patently glad to have her for a visitor. "I am full of alcohol and opium."

She approached, glancing at the bottle on the library table. "That's the laudanum." She checked it as closely as she might have an hourglass. "Why, it's nearly gone. Won't you need more? I can telephone the doctor."

"No. That will do."

"Do?"

"It will be enough."

"Oh."

"Sit down, please." He nodded at the armchair beside the bed and changed the subject. "Have you got any new roomers yet?"

She seated herself. "No. And I even ran an ad in the paper."

"That is my fault."

"Perhaps. It's probably the sight-seers across the street, too."

"They still come?"

"Every day. At first I thought they must be the town ne'er-do-wells, but I've recognized some of our best people. Cats can look at kings, you know—alley or pedigreed."

"Thibido said we should let them in and charge admission."

She smiled. "Not very likely. Oh, here, I'm forgetting why I came." She gave him a large envelope. "From Mr. Skelly."

He opened the envelope and eased out an eight-by-ten photograph. He stared at it.

"My God," he said.

She rose to look over his shoulder.

"My God," he said. "That's not me."

There he was, posed formally, standing against the flowered wallpaper, shoulders squared, hands in trousers pockets pulling back the lapels of the Prince Albert coat sufficiently to afford a glimpse of what hung in holsters on each side of the vest. And there they were, black handle and pearl, enough of each to titillate prosperity. He was a man of medium height. At the temples his brown hair was slashed with gray, as was the mustache

which drooped at the corners of his mouth. But it
was the face which shocked him. Fine-featured in
health, it had been as ravaged by disease as had
his body. It was cachectic. The skin, gray of cast,
was racked taut over the skull, bringing into hid-
eous prominence the bones of forehead, nose,
cheeks, and chin. The eyes were sunken, so that it
was impossible to tell what they considered, whether
an enemy, a straight flush, or the advent of a
civilization in which he must be anachronous.

"This is what I look like," he said, appalled.

"It must have been the artificial light," she con-
soled, sitting again. "And perhaps the paper, too.
I'm accustomed to tintypes."

Books continued to study it. After a minute he
opened the drawer of the library table, found a
pencil, turned the portrait over, wrote on the back,
and gave it to her.

"For you. Such as it is. It may be worth something someday."

"Why, how kind. I'm sure it will be. But isn't
there someone else you'd rather give it to?"

"No."

She turned the portrait over. "*For Mrs. Rogers
with regards,*" he had written, and signed it "*John
Bernard Books.*"

She did not trust herself to speak.

"I am sorry about the candy dish," he said. "I
was feeling low, and gave it a good heave. I have
smashed a lot of things in my life."

"It's—it's all right."

"No. I said I would not be a burden to you. So I
have shot two men in this room and chased your
roomers away and smashed some glassware already. Hostetler said one morning I will wake up

and not be able to get out of bed. Well, I promise not to let it go that far."

She got hold of herself. "I was delighted to see you had a lady caller yesterday. She asked me not to announce her—she wanted to surprise you. Were you surprised?"

"I was." He looked at her with a measure of amusement. "That's another thing about cats."

"What?"

"Curiosity kills them."

"If you think—"

"Her name is Serepta Thomas," he proceeded. "I lived with her for a time, eleven years ago. She left me for a freighter."

"Did you love her?"

"I did then. Now she is down and out. She asked me to marry her."

"She asked you?"

"Yes."

"Did she know about—I mean—"

"Yes. That was why she asked me. She wanted my name. And what money she could raise from it. Dobkins, the reporter, tracked her down in Tucson and had her come see me. He has a notion to write a book about me full of lies and put her name on it. Mrs. J. B. Books."

"That is despicable!" exclaimed Bond Rogers.

"No worse than the others. I am doing a land-office business these days. Skelly will be selling those pictures of me, and the undertaker intends to lay me out and show me to the public. For a price."

She was aghast. "You don't—you can't be serious!"

"I am."

"That is the most morbid, depraved—"

"There is one consolation. I am going to be a damn sight more popular dead than I have been alive."

She shook her head. "Men. And women, too. I don't know what the world is coming to. Let's not talk about it."

"All right."

The day was clouded, the room gloomy, the silence between them loud.

"How is the boy?" he asked.

"I've lost all control of him, frankly. Selling your horse was not only the most unprincipled thing he's ever done, it was actually criminal. I am stumped." She had forgotten how comforting it could be to talk to a man. It was a luxury she had been denied of late, and she let her words spill. "I can't discipline him, I can't afford to send him away, and if he doesn't soon reform himself, I can't tolerate living with him. I scarcely recognize Gillom as my son any more. He's a stranger to me. What would you do?"

"I told you. If you can, give him another father. The sooner the better."

She stirred. She longed to ask what had happened between them over the sale of the horse, in this room after she had left them together, but she did not dare. Guilt flooded her cheeks. She could not clear her mind's eye of Gillom in the parlor, on his knees, sobbing at the loss of a second father, nor exculpate herself for having been the one to tell him, to tell the secret with which she had been entrusted by a dying man.

"That's something else I would prefer not to discuss," she said, too sharply.

"Fair enough."

She was miserable. She cast about for a way to make amends. "There is a matter I've been meaning to say something about, Mr. Books." She resolved to be generous yet impersonal. "When you came, after you rented a room, I called you an 'assassin.' I regret that. I've thought about it a great deal. I realize now—the night those men came in the windows—they were here to kill you, and you had to defend yourself, anyone would. I mean, I realize now—this is how it must have been many times—you did not provoke the quarrels— men have always wanted to kill you. So I misused the world—I apologize—it is something about which I know very little—I have been sheltered— I never—"

She was in obvious distress. "By the way, Mrs. Rogers," he interjected, "my clothes are pretty roady. I would be much obliged if you could brush and press my coat and trousers. I will pay you for the time."

"Oh no," she demurred, thankful for the rescue. "I'd enjoy doing it. Are you sure you wouldn't rather have them cleaned?"

"Cleaned?"

"Yes, there's a new method now, called 'dry process cleaning.' We have several shops in El Paso."

"How long would it take?"

"They advertise next-day service. And the clothing looks like new—its miraculous. Why don't you let me have them now? I'll take them over myself, and you'll have them back tomorrow."

"I suppose I could," he said. "I am not going out. But I don't see—"

She sprang up, coloring. "I was leaving anyway.

I'll stand outside, and you hand them to me through the door."

"Very well."

Taking the portrait, she left the room and held the door ajar. Under his breath he cursed himself for requiring so long to get off the bed, get out of his trousers, get his coat from the closet, get to the door.

"Thank you," he said.

"You're very welcome."

As soon as the door closed, Books put a hand in the envelope on the bed, found the photographer's fifty dollars, and cached it in the top drawer of the chiffonier. He went then slowly, in dread, to the washbowl, to the mirror to which he had traded himself for his image every day while shaving. The man in the glass and the man in the portrait could not be one and the same. Either the mirror or the camera had cheated him. He stared.

The mirror had.

He heard the front door open, and Gillom Rogers, drunk perhaps, stumble up the stairs. It was well after midnight.

He thought: I would give anything to have her here, to talk to her. If only I had met her eleven years ago instead of Serepta. But it is too late to love her or let her love me. I am coming to the end of my rope. Besides, it would not be love on her part. It would be pity. I will be damned before I accept pity, from her or anybody.

He took up his newspaper. Except for the advertisements, there was little in it he had not read by now. One of these interested him. He read it twice:

Sweet Cream,
  Cream for coffee,
    Cream for oatmeal,
      Cream for applesause,
        Cream for ice cream.
I am now delivering cream on my wagon guaranteed with proper care to keep 24 hours after delivery. Telephone 156.
G. A. COBB
Proprietor, Missouri Dairy

A man named Steinmetz called on him the next day. He was shabbily dressed and spoke with an accent. He owned and operated an oddment emporium on San Antonio Street and might buy, he said, anything of a personal nature Books wished to sell, provided the asking price was not "outlandish." Books had him get his black valise from the closet and appraise the contents. There was a shirt, spare underwear, two pairs of socks, several handkerchiefs, a set of gold cuff links, and a bottle of hair tonic, in addition to the valise itself.

"Dis iss all?"

"That is all."

"But you are a man of middle age. To haf lived your life—to haf nuzzing—"

"I traveled light."

"Zo."

"I have a watch." He handed it over. "And my shaving things—razor, brush, mug. But I will need them."

"You could now sell dem to me," said Steinmetz. "You could a bill of sale sign, und I would get dem lader."

Books pulled at an end of his mustache. "And I would have the money now?"

"Vy nod?"

"How much?"

Steinmetz calculated. "Ten dollars?"

"Hell no. Fifty."

"Too much."

"That's a good watch. Gold case and a real diamond. And it is J. B. Books's watch. It will fetch double for that reason, and so will the rest, and you know it."

"Twenty dollars?"

"Fifty. For the lot."

"Some guns you haf."

"They are not for sale."

"Thirty?"

"Fifty."

Steinmetz rose. "Good day, Mr. Books." He bowed and left the room.

Seconds later someone knocked.

It was Steinmetz, hat in hand. "It iss true—you are dying, Mr. Books?"

"I am."

The secondhand man shook his head. He seemed on the verge of tears. "To haf lived zo long—to haf zo liddle. I am Chewish. I am a stranger in dis Texas, among too many *goyim*. I haf nod long from the Old Coundry come, but a wife I haf, und two sons, und my store, und already some land, und money in the bank. Yes, I will fifty dollars gif you."

Books looked out a window. He did not know whether to be offended by the comparison or gratified by the price. Part of that price was pity, he was sure—and he had sworn only last night not to accept it from anybody. Pain blurred his thinking. He wanted the fifty dollars desperately. It was not too dear for his possessions, but it assigned a pitifully low value to his pride. He swallowed it.

"Sold," he said.

He thought: Day after tomorrow.

Squatting, staring fixedly at the noble Indian on the wall who sat astride his pony and surveyed a wilderness with sorrowful mien, he strained, hoping the row of china cherubs along the rim of the slop-jar would strike up their harps in happy paean to his ability to piss. They did not. His bladder cramped. He was past the point of simple strangury. He could no longer urinate at all.

He thought: Day after tomorrow. I have difficulty walking now. My lower back will not allow me to sit or stand more than a spell. This was the first day I could not shave myself. Tonight, when she brought my supper tray, I was not hungry. I can't take anything in at one end or let loose of anything at the other. So, if I intend to go out with my boots on instead of in a stinking sickbed, it is day after tomorrow. The laudanum should see me through till then. If I asked Hostetler for more, it would be a temptation to hang on. Besides, I have started getting ready. When the solid citizens of El Paso line up to gawp at me, they will have their money's worth. Beckum will put a mean look on my phiz and my clothes will be cleaned by dry process. Now for the next step. A clean cadaver.

Taking a towel and washcloth, he went to the door, opened it, listened. The house was still. She would be asleep at this hour, the boy would be over on Utah Street going to hell as fast as he was able.

He limped along the dark hall to the bathroom, turned on a light, and ran hot water into the tub. When it was half full he tempered it with cold, then leaned against a wall to extricate himself from his longjohns, then bending, both hands on the edges of the tub, somehow got into it and groaning, lowered himself until he could sit submerged to the waist.

There was soap in a rack, and he washed himself where he could reach. The heat of the water seemed to allay the pain, was pleasing, in fact, to his genitals. He sank back, enjoying the sensation. But when he sat up, the bath had weakened him. Try as he might, he was unable to pull himself into a squat. He was helpless. He whimpered.

"Bond," he whimpered.

She would not hear him, he was trapped, far from his room and his drug. He would sit in the tub until he roared in agony like a bear.

"Bond!" he yelled in panic. "Bond!"

A sound on the ceiling, her springing out of bed, and in another moment he could follow her rapid footsteps down the stairs.

The door opened. She wore a flannel bathrobe. Her hair was up in rag curlers. "What in the world?"

"I can't get out."

"John, why in heaven's name didn't you ask me to help in the first place?"

"Because God damn it I can take my own bath!"

"Obviously you can't."

"I didn't want you to see me."

"Do you think I haven't seen a man before?"

"Hell."

"Have you washed your back?"

"How in hell could I?"

"Men are such infants." She came to the tub and soaped the washcloth. "Now lean forward."

"Hell."

"And stop swearing."

"Well, you haven't seen a man with cancer before."

"I have now." She scrubbed his back retributively. "Are you in pain?"

"All the time now."

"You should have told me you wanted a bath."

"I said I would not be a burden to you."

"Hush."

She pulled the stopper, laid a hand towel on the tub bottom so that he could stand securely on it and, bustling, bringing a large towel, dried his upper body. "Now, take my hands. I'll pull you up."

"Don't look at me."

Together, adding her strength to what remained of his, they got him into a crouch, then upright, and she assisted him out, wrapping him in the towel.

"We'll leave your underwear here," she said. "I'll wash it tonight and hang it and it'll be dry by morning. Now, put your arm around my waist. I'll help you back to bed."

They swayed down the hall, into his room. She laid back the covers, removed the towel and when he had sat down and stretched out, covered him again.

"The laudanum," he muttered.

She uncapped and handed it to him, and he drank. "Bond, stay with me a bit," he begged. "Till the stuff works."

"All right."

She sat down in the armchair beside him. The only light was a faintness emanating from the bathroom through the open door. They could scarcely see each other's faces.

"Ah, God," he sighed after a time.

"Better now?"

"Yes."

So quiet was it in the room that she could hear the ticking of his watch on the library table.

"I have come to a sad state of affairs," he said abruptly. "Just last night I told myself I would not take pity from anybody. Now I take anything they will give."

The rag curlers occurred to her. She began to untie them. "John."

"What?"

"You are getting ready—to do something, aren't you?"

"What makes you think that?"

"Having your things cleaned. Taking a bath. Letting the laudanum run down."

"I wish I had met you years ago."

"Aren't you?"

"Yes."

"It would be useless for me to inquire what."

"It would."

"You frighten me. I suppose I'd be more frightened if I knew."

"I will say this much. My life has not amounted to a damn-all. Maybe my death will."

"I see. May I ask a favor of you?"

"You may ask."

"Before you—before you do whatever it is—will you see my minister for a few minutes?"

"Why?"

"It may be that—that he can give you some comfort, some understanding. Some peace."

"I doubt it."

"It's possible. Will you for my sake? I want to do everything I can for you."

"You have done enough."

Suddenly she slipped from the chair and knelt and laid her head beside him.

"Oh, John, I will mourn for you!" she whispered. "You believe no one will—but I will! I'll remember your strength and your goodness and courage! I'll remember always!"

She was crying. He moved his fingers in her hair. "I will talk with the reverend," he said. "Provided you do one more thing for me."

"Anything!"

"Day after tomorrow," he said. "When you see me then, in my Sunday duds, there will be no tears."

She thought of armed men coming through these windows into darkness, of explosions like blows upon the door of doom, of blood staining her carpet and, soon, her heart. She shuddered.

"No tears, Bond."

"I promise."

"Day after tomorrow."


Unshaven, shirtless, in clean underwear and trousers cleaned by dry process, seated on his crimson pillow, Books received them.

"This is the Reverend Henry New, Mr. Books," she said. "Reverend, J. B. Books."

They shook hands.

"A pleasure to meet you, Mr. Books."

"Likewise."

"I'll leave you gentlemen now," Bond Rogers said. "It was kind of you to come, Reverend."

"It was my duty, Mrs. Rogers. Thank you for the opportunity."

When she had gone, Henry New took the straight chair. "How are you feeling today, Mr. Books?"

"As well as can be expected."

"I'm pleased to hear it. And I was sincere with Mrs. Rogers. I'm truly pleased to have an opportunity to meet a man of your—your distinction. A 'shootist'? I think that's the polite term."

" 'Killer' usually."

"Well, now that's somewhat crude. I'm sure you prefer 'shootist.' It has an elegance."

Books was unresponsive.

"A fine woman, Mrs. Rogers."

Books made a church of his fingers.

"She tells me you are—very ill."

"I am dying."

"I see. I regret profoundly to hear it. But you are not a young man. We can at least rejoice that God has granted you a fairly full measure. 'Thou shalt come to thy grave in a full age, like as a shock of corn cometh in his season.' "

Books had expected an older man, a Bible-bouncer, a deacon who would rant and roar and stomp the floor and take an errant soul by the scruff of the neck and throw it through the Pearly Gates as though they were swinging doors. That was the kind of preacher with whom he could cope, and from whom he might indeed gain a brimstone solace. To his dismay, Bond Rogers had sent him a ringer—a man not a day over thirty-two or -three, a bright-eyed, apple-checked, razor-brained whippersnapper first in his class at divinity school who could draw from the Old testament as fast as he, Books, could draw from his vest. He groaned inwardly. The last slug of laudanum was wearing off. He did not feel equal to the Reverend Henry New this morning.

"Do you believe in a life after death, Mr. Books?"

"I don't know."

"In a Heaven? In a Hell?"

"I don't know."

Henry New nodded. He seemed satisfied. "I confess to a certain perplexity in these matters myself. But of one thing I am positive. I know that God exists. I may not be a religionist, in the old-fashioned sense of the word, but I know, as surely as I know we sit here, that He exists, that I am His servant upon this earth, and that His wisdom is infinite. I prayed for you this morning, Mr. Books."

"Much obliged."

"As soon as Mrs. Rogers telephoned, I went to my study. I prayed, first, that God Our Father look with compassion upon His wayward son, John Bernard Books, and forgive his sins, and take him soon into that fold to which all men, great and small, aspire. That—"

"Sins?"

"I had reference to the killings."

"Hold on, Reverend. I have been in a tight or two, but they were not of my making."

His visitor raised a deprecatory hand. "Let us not debate the past, Mr. Books. My concern today is the future. I prayed this morning, second, for divine guidance. It struck me that with Mrs. Rogers' call I had been granted a unique opportunity. A man nearing his end, a man whose name was synonymous with profligacy and destruction—was

there not some way his demise might be used for
holy purposes? I prayed for vision, for a sign from
Him. And suddenly the scales fell from my eyes!
Eureka!" The minister's eyes burned like candles.
"I went immediately to my desk, Mr. Books. I
wrote as though Another's hand directed my pen!"
From an inner pocket of his coat he whisked a
folded paper. "Here!"

"What is it?"

"A statement from J. B. Books. To be read from
every pulpit in the land. A testimonial to the mercy
of Almighty God. Here, sir, read it."

Books would not take the paper. "No. You tell
me the particulars."

An annoyed Henry New twisted in his chair.
"Well, it's brief, and to the point and if I do say so
myself, eloquently phrased. In the main, it—"

Books scowled. "The particulars."

"Very well. You repent your misdeeds. You beg
the Lord's forgiveness." With each sentence he
tapped the paper impatiently on a knee. "In the
main, you address yourself to the younger genera-
tion of this country. You exhort them to profit by
your example. To take the high road rather than
the low. To practice continence, cultivate humility,
love virtue. To turn the other cheek rather than
resort to violence. To bear in mind that it is the
meek, not the proud, who shall inherit the earth.
Et cetera. Can you not appreciate how effective
such a document might be among the younger,
lawless element of our population?" He lowered
his voice confidentially. "If a Gillom Rogers, for
example, were to hear it, and to heed its lesson? I
need go no further." He proffered the paper a

second time. "I urge you to read and sign it, Mr. Books."

"No."

"What? You will not? Why not, sir?"

"Because it is a pile of shit."

Henry New's apple cheeks ripened. "I beg your pardon!"

"I never sit with my back to a door," Books added. "And I will not sign anything I do not believe in."

Frowning, the minister bit at a fingernail. "I can't believe you understand the consequences of refusal, Mr. Books. I have offered you a last chance to attest to the glory of God, to be an instrument of His will. To give your imminent death meaning."

"Meaning." Books grimaced. "The last two weeks every son of a bitch who walked into this room wanted something different out of my death. I am sick and tired of it."

"Ah, but you cannot ignore it!" countered the minister. "With every passing hour it becomes more prudent of you to lift your eyes unto the hills. Should you reconsider, and sign, I can practically guarantee your ultimate redemption."

Books's agony overwhelmed him. The last dose of the drug he had taken only a half hour earlier, and he was damned if he would exhibit his need for another, no matter how dire, before this bunkum artist.

"On the other hand," New warned, "should you persist in refusal, I tremble to predict the outcome. I caution you, sir—the fate of your very soul may be at stake. 'For God shall bring every work into judgment, with every secret thing, whether it be good, or whether it be evil.' "

Books could scarcely sit still. His spine cracked. The poison in his system suffused his limbs with heat. He wanted to whimper, to howl, or to take the pissant parson over his lap and spank the sanctimony out of him. His fingers tugged at the pillow tassels between his legs. "I will take my chances," he choked. "At least I will see my cards sooner than you—and I will bet my hand is as good as yours."

The Reverend New tucked away his statement and ascended from his seat. "Sir, I did not come here to be insulted by a man of your ilk."

"No—you came here to comfort me—like hell you did! You came here full of opportunity and crap!"

New proceeded to the door. He turned. To his astonishment, to his almost sensual pleasure, Books's cheeks were wet. The minister permitted himself a tremor of self-esteem. If he had not beaten the assassin at his own game of bluff and threat, if he had not cast this Devil Incarnate into the pit of contrition, he had at least reduced him to tears.

"You are lost, Mr. Books," he sniffed. "I wash my hands of you."

"Oh, Preacher," cried his archenemy, "if I had my strength, wouldn't I boot your hypocritical ass out of here!"

"Piffle." New adjusted his tie, regarding with infinite contempt the shambles of a man who sat playing with the tassels of a pillow. "Good morning, sir. I leave you to your alcohol and opium."

"And my death!" Book sobbed. "You leave my death to me!"

He sobbed to himself. Henry New had gone.

\*      \*      \*

He thought: Tomorrow.

It had taken him two hours and two long pulls at the laudanum bottle and two chasers of whiskey to recover from the minister's visit. He knew now that he was very near the bottom of the well, both physically and emotionally. The disease, the pain, the confinement, the loneliness, had finally undone him. He could no longer trust that steel self upon whom he had relied, in a pinch, for so many haphazard years. It must be tomorrow. And in the early afternoon he sent for Gillom Rogers.

"Close the door."

Gillom closed it, staring at the man on the bed. He had not seen Books for days. He had never seen such a face.

"Tell me. Which is the best saloon in El Paso? I mean, the one with the most class."

"That's easy. The Connie."

"Connie?"

"The Constantinople. It's brand new. Oh, it's jim dandy. They really spent the spondulix on that one."

"All right. Now tell me something else. Do you know a man named Pulford?"

"Sure. Runs the faro layout at Keating's. They say he's sent a couple to Kingdom Come. Is he slick, is he fast. Wouldn't I like to see him and Jay Cobb go to it, though."

"What about Cobb?"

"Hay? He's a pal of mine. He's hiding out now, but I know where."

"Hiding out?"

"I'll say. Thibido let him out of the *juzgado* the other night. He went to Tillie Howard's and got drunk and hurt one of her girls and got thrown out and then tried to gun down the rest of the girls. Thibido's looking for him. He won't bring him in on his feet, though, not Jay." Gillom's ears itched now. "Why?"

"Is there somebody named Serrano?"

"Cross-eye? What a plug-ugly he must be. Rustles cattle. I've never set eyes on him, but I think he hangs out across the river. Say, what's this all about?"

"I want you to do something for me. Pulford, Cobb, Serrano. Find them. Go to each one and tell him I will be in the Constantinople at four o'clock tomorrow afternoon."

"Hey." Gillom sat down on the edge of the straight chair. "Hey."

"Just don't mention to any of them I have invited the others. And don't tell anybody else."

"Oh my God." Gillom hugged himself with excitement. "I get it. Oh Jesus."

"Four o'clock. Do they know about me?"

"That you're a goner? Everybody in town does. Jesus!" Gillom jumped up, tangled his large feet, and fell happily against the chiffonier. "I get it! They save you the trouble of doing yourself in! They do it for you! Oh, that's a peach!"

"The Constantinople."

Gillom propped an elbow on the chest. "O.K. I'll do it. Might not be easy tracking Cross-eye down, but I will, you bet. Say, what do I get for this?"

"What do you want?"

"You know."

"Well?"

Gillom licked his lips rather than chewing them. He liked the taste of himself much better now. "I want your guns."

"No."

"No? Then send somebody else. Send Thibido. Send my ma. You've got no choice."

"Don't ask for my guns."

"I ain't asking, I'm telling. I could take 'em right this minute, and you couldn't lift a finger. So it's the guns or go to hell, Mister J. B. Books. Or lay here and die by yourself. Or go over to the Connie and scare those hard cases to death. With your face, you could."

Books closed his eyes. "All right. They're yours. Later."

"Damn right they are. About five minutes past four tomorrow. Maybe not even that long."

"Hop to it, then," Books said. "And don't job me, boy."

Gillom grinned. "I won't. I wouldn't miss the looks on their faces. Oh Jesus."


The day warmed.

That afternoon he opened the windows and let warm wind blow the curtains and heard again the wheels of the streetcar as it passed the corner.

Two sweating men in dungarees delivered the headstone from Beckum, the undertaker. It was covered by a canvas, and Books was careful that Bond Rogers admitted the men and left the room before he uncovered it. The marble seemed to be of good quality, and the inscription had been cut as specified: "*John Bernard Books 1849-1901.*" He had the draymen place it against the wall and when they had gone draped it with his Prince Albert coat so that she would not see it.

He then brought his Remingtons and bullets

from the closet and, lying on the bed, cleaned the guns and reloaded, filling the sixth chamber in each.

Gillom entered, without knocking, just before suppertime, and found him asleep, Remingtons beside him. He tiptoed to the bed but no sooner had the youth picked up one of the guns than Books awoke. He put out a hand. Gillom gave him the weapon.

"Not yet," Books said.

"Not long," Gillom said.

Books pushed a pillow upright behind his shoulders. "Well?"

"I told them."

"What did they say?"

"Pulford nothing. Jay nothing. I had to go across the river to Juárez to find Serrano. He's got a wife and a whole litter of kids—they were crawling all over the place. I told him the Connie, four o'clock tomorrow. Then I got out of there fast." Gillom frowned. "The thing is, none of 'em said a word. I don't know if they'll really show."

"They'll show."

"Who says?"

"They are small men."

"Small hell. They're fast. I know for a fact Jay and Pulford are, and Cross-eye's mean as sin."

"One deals. One drives a creamery wagon. One rustles cattle. They are small potatoes, and this is the best chance they will ever have to be big. They will show."

"Maybe."

"Now you can do two more things for me."

"Not for you. For the guns."

"Send me a barber in the morning. And shine my boots tonight."

In the moonlight through the windows he squinted at his watch, the watch he had already sold to Steinmetz. It was after one o'clock.

He thought: Today.

He pulled on the lamp, drank from the laudanum bottle, and estimated three fingers remained. It would see him through, although it afforded him only the most fleeting respite now. He had not urinated for thirty-six hours, and he had slept this night, fitfully, in the leather armchair for fear he would be incapable of getting out of bed in the morning.

He took up the *Daily Herald* for Tuesday, January 22, 1901, the day he had ridden into El Paso. The paper was dry and brittle. He had read everything in this edition, all eight pages, every news story, every advertisement, every joke, every line of filler. For once he had got the whole good out of a newspaper. For lack of anything else to do, he reread an item on the front page in the column centered under the great black headlines:

London, Jan. 22—The Privy Council has drawn up the proclamation announcing the accession of Edward Prince of Wales, to the throne. The royal apartments in Buckingham Palace are being made ready for the reception of the court. Members of Parliament are arranging to meet in special session. The funeral arrangements are planned. The theaters are scheduled to close for at least a week. Dressmakers and ladies' tailors are fairly swamped with orders countermanding colored costumes and ordering mourning gowns. Hatters are laying in a big stock of deep hatbands. Stationers are getting mourning edge stationery. Drapers are being employed, and all are rushed with work. Orders have been prepared prescribing the period of mourning for all the official departments, the diplomatic and consular service, and the army and navy at home and abroad.

He folded the newspaper and placed it on the rack under the library table.

He thought: Well, Victoria, Your Royal Highness, old lady, old girl, we are about to get together. I will not make as big a splash as you did. I do not expect they will sell much drape, but there may be a minute of silence in the saloons. I have never read what a man is supposed to do when he is presented to you. Kiss your hand, I imagine. But you will know a gent when you meet him, you will recognize blood as blue in a way as yours. I will show you my guns, if you like, and we will drink tea and talk. You were the last of your kind, and they say, Dobkins and Thibido, that I am the last of mine, so we have a hell of a lot in common. I see by the paper they have made a smart of money out of you turning up your toes. Well, they are trying to do the same with me. Your life meant considerable, I guess, and mine did not, but maybe my death will. We will see shortly. Maybe we did outlive our time, maybe the both of us did belong in a museum—but we hung onto our pride, we never sold our guns, and they will tell of the two of us that we went out in style. So today, old girl, a hair after four o'clock, at the palace. You be dressed in your best bib and tucker, Vickie, and so will I.

Deciding to drink to his impending audience with the Queen, he groaned himself out of the chair to the closet, opened the bottle, changed his mind, and poured the last of the whiskey into the washbowl. He would let today stand on its own two legs.

As he sat down again, the pain receding, the third line of the poem recited itself to him: "For he on honey-dew hath fed . . ."

He thought: Oh, I have fed on honey-dew. On wine and whiskey and champagne and the tender white meat of women and fine clothes and the respect of strong men and the fear of weak and the turn of a card and good horses and the crisp of greenbacks and the cool of mornings and all the elbow room that God or man could ask for. I have had high times. But the best times of all were afterward, just afterward, with the gun warm in my hand, the bite of smoke in my nose, the taste of death on my tongue, my heart high in my gullet, the danger past, and then the sweat, suddenly, and the nothingness, and the sweet clean feel of being born.

# Five

The barber's name was Gigante.

He nodded, he smiled, he nodded, he smiled, but could not utter a word. He was terrified. When, in the process of shaving, he applied a cold towel rather than a hot, and Books let out an oath, he jumped. Books ordered him to trim his mustache, and the hair in his nose, and the hair in his ears. After shearing the gun man's long hair, Gigante took from the pocket of his white jacket a whisk broom, brushed the clippings from his customer's shoulders to the carpet, got down on hands and knees, brushed the clippings on the carpet into a pile, took a paper sack from another pocket, brushed the pile of clippings into the paper sack, and rising, clutched the sack to his chest.

"How much do I owe you?" Books asked.

Gigante could scarcely speak. "Dollar."

"You owe me ten."

"Ten?"

"For that sack of J. B. Books's hair. You will sell it for twenty. So give me ten."

The barber dropped the sack, gave him ten, picked up the sack.

"Thank you," said Books.

"Thank," said Gigante.

It was noon. He would have liked to inspect himself in the mirror to see what the barber had done, but that would mean getting out of the chair and going to the mirror, and he had to hoard himself. Judging that there was enough drug left to put him under till two o'clock, he drained the bottle. He had been unable to take nourishment for a day and a half, and he had told his landlady not to bother with lunch for him. He lay down on the bed.

He heard hoofs. Leaping from the brush, he leveled a Remington at the rider and ordered him to throw down his wallet. The man was thin and elderly and had a claw hand for a left hand, cocked perpetually at the wrist, the fingers stiff and splayed. Reining up, he reached inside his shirt. Books waggled his gun in warning. "I ain't armed," the rider croaked. "You be careful of that nickel-plate." Slipping a purse from inside his shirt, he tossed it. Books let his eyes follow, and therefore did not see the antiquated cap-and-ball pistol which appeared suddenly in the horseman's good hand, nor did he hear the explosion because the bullet exploded in his abdomen, crazed through the vitals, was deflected by the spine, and lodged, spent, in the socket of his left hip. He dropped the Remington and fell to his knees.

"My God, you've murdered me!"

"Bring me my purse."

"I can't! My God!"

"Bring it, you young bastard, or I'll put another one through the same hole."

One hand grasping the purse, the other stopping his stomach as though it were a barrel with the bung out, and blubbering, staggering to the horseman, Books handed up the purse.

"Thankee," said the rider, putting away purse and weapon and taking reins.

"You won't leave me here!"

"Won't I?" The old jasper considered him. "I'll do you a favor, though. You've got a bellyache you ain't a-going to get shet of. You can die slow or now. If you hanker, I'll kill you."

"Kill me!"

"If'n I was in your fix, I'd be obliged. I'm a fair shot, as you see, and you look to me as if you've sucked the front tit long enough."

Books backed off and sank to his knees again and began to wail like a child. His mouth hung open in shock. Saliva dripped from his chin.

"Suit yourself," said Claw Hand, turning as he rode on. "Don't try to hold nobody else up before you die, Sonny. You ain't worth a damn at it."

His wails and the spittle on his chin woke him. It was past three o'clock, not two.

He hauled himself off the bed and began to dress as rapidly as the damage done to his innards by the old man's bullet would allow.

He put on the white shirt she had washed and ironed, and the gray bow tie. Back to the wall, he tugged on his pants, then sat down again to grapple with socks and the black lizard boots the boy had shined.

That done, he stood before the mirror and contrived, without acknowledging in the glass that ghastly stranger who claimed to be kin to him, to run a comb through his hair and his mustache.

His vest, which he got from the closet, hung too loosely about his ribs. The guns sagged. He had lost that much weight. Cursing under his breath, opening and banging shut the drawers of the chiffonier, he found a safety pin, removed the vest, and pinned a fold in the back, then put it on again and was satisfied. He wound his watch and dropped it in a vest pocket.

He next put on his black Prince Albert coat, in so doing uncovering the headstone. Opening the top drawer of the chiffonier, he took out the money cached there, brought it to the library table, and sat down. There were two hundred dollars from his horse, the photographer's fifty, and undertaker's forty, fifty from Steinmetz, and ten from the barber. Emptying his wallet except for a dollar—that and the nickel in his pants would be sufficient, he was sure, unto the day—he added the bills to those on the table and counted. The total came to $532. That was what he had to show for his half century: five hundred-odd dollars. He had won more than that up in Oklahoma once, in one hand, on a pair of treys. From the table drawer he took the envelope and sheet of paper he had asked of her the preceding day, telling her he might send a letter to a friend. Using the table top as surface, he penciled a note:

Mrs. Rogers:
Use this money and send the boy away to school. See that Beckum bureys me proper and uses my headstone. I have sold my things to the secondhand man so give them to him.

Folding the sheet around the money, he stuffed it in the envelope, licked the flap and sealed the envelope, and standing, placed it upright against the back of the armchair.

He stepped to the center of the room. Raising his right hand and arm, sliding the hand inside his coat, he drew the Remington from its holster on his left side: once, twice, thrice. He did not try for speed but for fluidity of movement, the arm rising naturally, the fingers closing easily and surely about the handle, the withdrawal smooth, the entire gesture as unstudied and reflexive as though he had reached for and brought forth a cigar. He then did likewise with the Remington on his right side: once, twice, thrice.

He went to the closet, got his gray Stetson, blew dust from the brim, reshaped the crease, tried the hat on, took it off.

Picking up the crimson velvet pillow he had stolen from the whorehouse in Creede, Colorado, he moved slowly to the door, and for a moment rested his forehead against it, dizzy with exertion. Under his longjohns he was dripping wet. He tried to calculate the number of days this room had been his home but could not. He peered sideways, at a framed picture on the wall. The setting was a woodland glade, and a tranquil pool about which, gazing at their reflections in the pool, knelt several nymphs, clad just diaphanously enough to reveal their rather buxom charms. They were not alone. Spying upon them from the foliage was a gang of half-men, half-goats, with horns and hoofs and hairy legs and tails, who appeared to him to be working up a lust to leap and lay hell out of the nymphs.

He thought: Nobody will ever believe I could have done this today and neither by God will I.

He left the room.

Had he turned and looked around it a last time, he might have noticed the shadow in the lace curtains at the west window.

He entered the Constantinople at three forty-one, having sneaked through alleys and side streets to avoid encountering the marshal or his deputies. He wanted ample time to make ready. Since the saloon was new, it had developed little patronage as yet. There were only two men at the bar, and the barkeep. He walked to the bar, bought a shot of whiskey, and carried it with him to the left rear corner of the room. Here he stood, uncertain whether to sit in one of the three wine booths built into the corner or at a table. It occurred to him that the walls of a booth might obstruct his vision, if not of the front doors, then of the archway at rear center, which opened into the gambling room, and he seated himself therefore at a corner table in front of the booths. From this vantage he would have the front doors in full view and could keep an eye, at least peripherally, on the archway.

He cupped the butt of each Colt's, one holster tied to his left thigh, one to his right. He was ready, whatever that meant. The knowledge of gunplay he had accumulated in his twenty years was scant, as it was of girls and kings and arithmetic and cows and prayer and mountains and everything except how to draw and fan and fire a revolver unerringly and how to hate himself and how to deliver milk and cream and butter. He touched a pustule on his neck. He would not have bet a dime of the money he had taken from his father that Books would actually show up at four o'clock, but as he lifted the glass to his lips, so palsied was his hand that he spilled some of the whiskey. It was not fear. It was an almost childlike hope—hope that this first, this best, perhaps this only chance he would ever have to distinguish himself in any way would not elude him, that the great assassin would in fact appear, and that he, Jay Cobb, could shoot him dead.

Hat in hand, pillow under arm, he stopped in the entry, facing the parlor.

"Mrs. Rogers," he said.

She rose too swiftly from the sofa. She had waited there for him, seeing nothing, hands folded in her lap, counting with the clock, all afternoon.

"How grand you look," she smiled.

"Thank you. So do you."

"Thank you."

They kept that formal distance from each other which may be more intimate than an embrace.

"Dry process cleaning is—is very good, isn't it?" she asked.

"Yes. It is smelly, though."

"That's the naphtha."

"The naphtha."

The clock ticked. She knew what it had required of him to dress himself, to leave his room. He knew how close she was to the tears he had forbidden. Silently, each entreated of the other a sacrifice, and a grace, which was humanly impossible.

"I am going to a saloon to have a drink," he said, taking masculine initiative. "I have not been out for a long time."

"How nice," she smiled. "Indeed you haven't. And you have a beautiful day for it. It's very warm. We're having what we call 'false spring.' "

"Oh?"

This exchange left them mute again. Her words to him, on the day of his arrival, worked like worms within the darkness of her soul: "I'm glad you're not staying long, Mr. Hickok. I don't believe I like you." And later: "You are a vicious, notorious individual utterly lacking in character or decency." For his part, he recalled with chagrin his underestimate of her at the beginning. The West was filling up with women like her, he had observed to himself, and he would not give a pinch of dried owl shit for the lot of them. Trapped in self-reproach, each deferred to the other.

Unexpectedly he put out his hand. "Good afternoon, Mrs. Rogers."

Their fingers met but did not twine.

"Good afternoon, Mr. Books."

He opened the door and, for the first since he had gone for a drive in the country with mother and son, stepped into the world.

He blinked. Light blinded him. Din deafened him—the rumble of a wagon, voices, a train whistle in the distance. He stood bewildered. Finally he put on his Stetson, and holding the pillow tightly under an arm, moved cautiously across the porch to the steps. He paused. He must descend them. He had left the house door open. He must not waste himself going back to close it. He squinted. The street corner he judged to be nine rods away. Weak as he was, and drenched with sweat, and in such pain that he ground his teeth together till they squeaked, he could walk nine rods.

He descended the steps—one and—two and—three and—four and—five; then paused again on the wooden sidewalk. The nape of his neck told him she was watching from a window.

He started. Once he had unlocked his legs, once he heard the familiar cadence of his boot heels on the sidewalk slats, once he was convinced he could indeed negotiate the nine rods, he opened himself as wide as he had the door of the house and let the world in. The day was buoyant. A ship of tropic air had voyaged inland from the Gulf of Mexico with a freight of spices, and this day on the desert was informed with a balm and sensuality that made him long to cry out, not with pain but with delight. He could not remember an afternoon more beautiful than this. It seemed to him that he had never before been so alive.

He reached the corner in two jerks of a lamb's tail, or thought he did, and waited there, nodding approbation of his feat as old men nod.

A little girl, her hair done up in ribbons, trotted along the street, rolling a hoop before her.

"Good day, madam," he said, and doffed his hat, and bowed.

She caught the hoop and stared at him, then gasped and ran away, frightened, clutching her hoop. It was his cachectic face.

Waiting, he listened. After a time it came to him, the high ringing sound, iron on iron, like that of clapper on bell, louder now, and drawing nigh.

Gillom Rogers climbed through the west window and made straight for the armchair. He tore

open the envelope, unfolded the sheet of paper. He
read the note to his mother. He counted the money,
grinning. Then, putting money in one pants pocket,
envelope and note in the other, he climbed out the
window and skulked along the back of the house,
turned, and stationed himself at a point from which
he could spy on the corner and the man there.

Serrano, or *El Tuerto,* or Cross-eye, as he was
more often called, entered the Constantinople at
three fifty-one, accompanied by a man named
Koopmann. There was a man at the bar, and the
barkeep, and a pimply kid wearing two guns seated
at a table in front of the wine booths at the left rear
corner of the saloon. Serrano and Koopmann stepped
to the bar and bought a drink. The barkeep was
barely civil to them, his attitude implying that the
Constantinople catered to a better class of patrons.
On another occasion the pair might have taken
umbrage at the slight, but they had bigger fish to
fry this day.

Serrano chose a table dead center of the room,
back to the wall. Koopmann sat beside him. Cross-
eye pulled a Peacemaker from his belt and laid it
in his lap, while Koopman did likewise with a
Navy Colt's. Koopmann had for some time had
business associations with Serrano, and the latter
had enlisted his support this afternoon on both
material and personal grounds. If he, Serrano, were
laid low, he had argued, Koopmann was incapable
of rustling cattle successfully by himself, so it be-
hooved him to see that he, Serrano, retained his
health and his acumen. His personal reasons *El
Tuerto* put as logically. Some gringo cattlemen
had recently declared their intention to kill him if

he did not kill J. B. Books if J. B. Books did not kill him. And since he did not care to chance being killed by J. B. Books, notwithstanding the celebrated gunman's physical condition or state of mind, or by the gringo cattlemen for that matter, he declared his intention to kill Koopmann if he, Koopmann, did not assist him in killing J. B. Books.

They sipped whiskey. Koopmann, a big, clean-shaven man, wore flowered suspenders and a derby hat. Serrano watched the front doors with his right eye and with his left, the exotropic, watched Jay Cobb.

The streetcar turned the corner a block away and, like a small boat upon a lazy river, glided in dignity toward him, drawn by a somnolent mule yclept Mandy by all El Pasoans. The car was small, seating but twelve passengers, and painted bright yellow with black trim and lettering: TRANVIAS DE CIUDAD JUAREZ above the windows, the numeral *1* in the center, and EL PASO & JUAREZ along the side. Exit was over a platform at the rear, entrance at the front, up two steps onto a platform where the boatman, or conductor, sat upon a three-legged stool, sombrero over eyes, reins in one hand, cash-box beside him.

As though it knew he wished to board, the street-car stopped. Books mounted the platform, noted the "5¢" on the box, located the nickel in his pocket, and dropped the fare.

"I want to go to the Constantinople."

This was too many syllables for the conductor, a Charon of advanced years and innumerable miles behind the mule.

"The Connie?" Books tried.

"Ah. Con-nee. *Si, señor.*"

Books entered the car and, placing his pillow upon the bench, seated himself. There were no other passengers. The conductor clucked, the car moved.

He had never ridden on a streetcar and, had it not been for his suffering, might have enjoyed this modern means of transport. The mule plodded, the roadbed was smooth, the roll of four iron wheels upon iron rails produced a not unpleasant monotone. On his stool the driver dozed, reins in hand, resting in peaceful certitude that neither buggy nor bicycle nor eccentricity of nature would stay his partner from the slow but sure completion of his appointed rounds. It seemed spring, but it was not, for the mulberry trees along the street did not as yet show bud.

The car stopped, and another passenger boarded, paid her fare, and seated herself near Books but opposite. She was dainty, and blond, in her middle twenties, and he believed her at once the loveliest girl he had ever seen. He twisted sideways and put an elbow out the window, the better to admire her. There was dew upon her lips; under his gaze her lashes beat like wings. She wore a long dress of lavender silk, with leg o' mutton sleeves. White lace foamed from her cleavage to her throat and garnished her skirt. She crossed her legs, affording him a glimpse of white stocking, a shapely ankle, and white high-button shoes. Adorning her blonde tresses was a hat of white straw which bloomed with lavender carnations. She carried a white parasol upon which no drop of rain would presume to fall. She could have been the darling of the town's most affluent family or the costliest jewel of a parlor house—it was impossible to say. To the critical observer, her beauty might have been flawed by the livid bruise upon her cheek, but only a little.

A block behind the streetcar Gillom Rogers followed, keeping interval with steady pace.

Since the afternoon was unseasonably warm, the doors were open and, entering the Constantinople, Jack Pulford stopped short.

The barkeep looked at him, then at Jay Cobb, then at Serrano and Koopmann, then at Pulford again, and aware, suddenly, that an event of some enormity was about to take place upon his premises, froze, glass in hand, polish cloth in glass.

The gambler stood almost at attention. The Constantinople was new, prices were higher than elsewhere, and he had expected to have the saloon, except for the barkeep, to himself. The three patrons looked at him, recognized him. He looked at them. The young two-gun tough he did not recognize, nor the man in the derby. Serrano he did. He took in their positions, too, relative to the doors behind him, to the archway at the rear, and to each other. He reflected. Maturity whispered that discretion was the better part of valor, impulse shouted to turn and walk out while there was time. Instead, having made a choice, he stepped left and took a chair at a table in the front so that he had a full sweep of the room.

To cover his apprehension, he examined his fingernails. He smoothed a sleeve of his white silk shirt. He weighed, and decided against, having a drink. He slipped and reholstered the Smith & Wesson on his right hip and was conscious that his palm was damp and reflected on that. Jack

Pulford had come to the Constantinople willingly. He had felt at first that his own, earlier statement, prompted by what to him was a justifiable vanity, had left him no alternative. "There was a man," he had said to a full faro table with reference to J. B. Books, "I could've beat." And when the Rogers kid had delivered the challenge from Books before another full table therefore, he was caught in a squeeze chute: put up or shut up, make good his mouth or go crawl. But last night, pondering Books's motive, trying to divine his hole card, he had finally sorted out the hand. What he had received was not a challenge but an invitation, a plea almost, for help. Books seemed to be saying, Look, I am cashing in, chip by chip, and I am squeamish about hurrying matters along by myself, so meet me tomorrow at four o'clock and do my killing for me. I have heard there is no better man in west Texas for the job. So meet me at four, Pulford, and write your name in the history books. No one will remember that I was on my last legs, no one will suspect. All they will remember is that J. B. Books was faced and killed in a saloon in El Paso in 1901 by one Jack Pulford. That was it, that was the reason, the gambler satisfied himself. What else could a dying man possibly desire beyond a dose of merciful lead?

So he had arrived as invited, ready to do business, and now this—a marked deck if he had ever seen one. If all Books wanted was an execution, why swell the guest list, why ask a drooling, double-gun idiot and low characters like Cross-eye and Derby Hat to the affair? They were obviously waiting for four o'clock, as he was. It made no damned sense.

He drew his watch. He would soon have an answer. It was three fifty-five.

Jack Pulford shot his cuffs. The Constantinople suited his taste to a *t*. In a day or two, he resolved, he would find out who had financed it and inquire what they would pay a faro dealer with his style.

He glanced at the other three again, with disdain. He would win anyone's money, that was his profession, but when it came to high stakes, to life or death, he favored the company of his peers.

The streetcar halted. The conductor pointed across the street. "Con-nee," he said.

"Thank you."

Books attempted to stand and lift the crimson pillow with him so that he would not have to stoop for it, but could not. When on his feet, he bent at the knees, picked it up, and took it to the forward platform, to the conductor.

"For you," he said.

The Mexican did not get his intention. Books gestured at the stool.

"Ah!" The conductor accepted the pillow, placed it on the stool, and sat down again, smiling. "*Es muy grande! Gracias, señor!*"

Books turned and moved back through the car, toward the exit platform. But rather than passing the lovely girl in lavender and white, he paused and removed his hat. He swayed.

"Will you rise, ma'am?" he asked.

She had been conscious of his admiration during the ride, had watched him as he presented the pillow to the conductor, but she looked at him bravely now for the first time, at his face, the face from which a child had fled, and drew breath. She rose. Her eyes filled.

She knew.

He took her in his arms and kissed her long and ardently. Men in their hosts, young and old, innocent and corrupt, had paid her for her favors, but she put her arms about him of her own free will as though to give him what she could in recompense for this, the last gift she guessed, of his manhood.

He let her go and walked drunkenly to the rear of the car, to the platform, and put on his hat, and stepped down, one and, two and, felt the ageless earth beneath his boots.

It was three fifty-eight.

He thought: I will make them wait on me a little. It is such a beautiful afternoon.

He leaned against a brick building, one of the largest in town, the recently constructed Myar Opera House. Beside him, a framed poster announced a concert that night by the El Paso Symphony Orchestra. The program would include, so he read, selections from Balfe's *Bohemian Girl*, Mascagni's *Intermezzo Sinfonico*, and Von Flotow's overture to *Stradella*.

He thought: When I walk in there, they will think there is a lot of me to kill. They will be wrong. Tarrant owns my horse and saddle. The barber has bought my hair. The secondhand man will have my watch and such, my guns will go to the boy. The photographer has my likeness. My cancer, and my corpse, belong to Beckum. That reporter did not get my reputation, though. Serepta cannot sell my name. And the reverend went away without my soul. So I have kept my valuables.

They will not be wrong after all, then, the three of them. There is still a lot of me to kill.

Down the street, hiding in the doorway of a small cigar manufactory, Gillom Rogers waited, watched. Now and then he touched a trousers pocket as though to reassure himself that the money was there.

A bolt of pain sheered through Books from hip to hip. He was stricken by a paroxysm of such terrible intensity that his knees buckled, that he clawed at the brick behind him with his fingers to keep from falling, that he clenched his jaws to keep from screaming in the street. Counterpoint to the pain, all four lines played through his mind in perfect harmony and tempo: "Weave a circle round him thrice/And close your eyes with holy dread/For he on honey-dew hath fed/And drunk the milk of Paradise."

He thought: Well. I am fifty-one years old and I have finally learned some poetry.

He checked his watch again. It was four-two. He put his back to the brick and stood erect and brought both arms close in to his ribs, and closer, until he had the fellowship of the guns. Then, through the sunlight of his pride, under the shadow of his agony, J. B. Books crossed the street and entered the Constantinople.

# Six

He thought: Let them gawp. Let them conclude you do not give a good God damn.

It was the right place. The Constantinople had more class than any saloon he had ever seen, and would deserve its fame. The barroom was long, with a ceiling twenty feet high, and suspended from it were four three-balded fans which revolved slowly, cooling the room on this warm day, and which were powered, probably, by electricity. The floor was a mosaic of green and white tiles. The woodwork—bar, tables, chairs, wine booths—was mahogany bleached to a reddish hue and carved with intricate Moorish designs. The bar was perhaps thirty feet long, and fronting the mirror behind it, on shelves, were tiers of sparkling glassware sized and shaped for every libation, for whiskey, and beer, for champagne and wine and liqueurs. The cash register gleamed, as did the bar rail, as did the cuspidors, as did the light fixtures, which were grapes of glass. Each table top was inset with shell and beadwork in stars and crescent moons. Beyond the bar, this side of the archway, was a billiard table. Inside the doors, to the right, was a mahogany booth, with a door of frosted glass and gilt littering: *"Telephone."*

It was the murals, however, the scope and subject matter of the murals, which stunned. They covered the walls, that over the bar, over the archway, and the full wall to the left. They depicted, in colors that whooped, in perspective that was fantastically out of whack, exotic scenes on the far side of exotic seas. There were domes and mosques and caravans of camels and pyramids and horsemen waving scimitars and minarets and palm trees and Sphinxes and tombs and dancing girls with navels as big as the tops of tin cans and boobs as pendant as hams hung on hooks and tents and oases on burning sands and dhows on rivers and dusty battles. The Constantinople had class, all right, but Books was in some doubt about the murals. They appeared to be the masterwork of a frontier genius who had been paid in alcohol or opium and who, by the time he had slap-dashed his visions and laid down his brush, had become either an addict or an irredeemable drunk. They spit in the rational eye. They kicked art in the ass.

He thought: Well, it will not be where I was that will count. It will be what I did.

Only then, after he had looked his fill, only then did Books acknowledge the existence of the others. Jay Cobb he could identify by his youth; Serrano by his plug-ugliness; Pulford by his attire and dealer's hands. The man in flowered suspenders and derby hat, Cross-eye's side-kick, he could not. One by one he considered them. He sensed their awe of him, and their unease. They knew why he had come, or believed they did, but none of the three principals, Cobb or Serrano or Pulford, understood why in hell the other two were here. And in their turn they stared at him, and waited, motionless, and stared. They were like actors on an empty stage, the five. The curtain had risen, the hour come. But they had no audience, save for one another, and even more bewildering, they had no play. They were assembled to take roles for which no lines had yet been written, to participate in a tragedy behind which there was no clear creative intent, to impose upon senselessness some sort of deadly order.

Books gave them a cue. Stepping to the center of the bar, boot heels clicking on the tile, he turned his back to them.

The barkeep slid along the bar to him, treading on eggs. He was a long drink of water called "Mount" Murray, and he had moved from the Acme to the Constantinople when the latter opened. The wages were better, the atmosphere higher-toned. Murray had noted them enter, first the four, now the man who must be J. B. Books. What he was about to witness he could not imagine, except that it would be slaughterous, and every instinct clamored that on the floor or under the billiard table or any damned where in that room would be a damned dangerous place to be.

"Sir?" he said.

"I will have a glass of white wine," said Books.

"Yes, sir."

The barkeep poured a glass, and when he set it on the bar Books put down his dollar bill. Murray did not seem to see it. He about-faced and strode along the bar past the billard table and through the archway with as much dignity as his ladder-legs would allow.

Books was alone. Using his left hand, resting his right on the bar near the opening between the lapels of his Prince Albert coat, he sipped the wine. He faced the mirror, in which was reflected the entire panorama of the room behind him, and its occupants.

He thought: Watch now, Victoria, watch. We are checking to each other now, which is a word we use in poker, a game of cards, but any second one of them will bet. One of them, Your Majesty, will make a move.

Waiting, surveying the room in the mirror through an opacity of pain, he could accept at last the horror of his countenance. This was the face the world would see tomorrow, at the undertaker's, after it had paid its fifty cents. It would have its money's worth tomorrow, and tomorrow night, bad dreams.

He thought: I do not know which one it will be, or what will happen, but neither do they. So we start even. No, not even, they are well and I am not. But I have an edge too. They want to live.

It was silent in the Constantinople. And yet, threaded through the silence was a breathing, a soft and rhythmic respiration. It was the fans overhead, turning slowly, easing the stale and anxious air.

He thought: All right, you sons of bitches. I have given you your chance, now give me mine. Give me some meaning. Let's go.

Rising at his table in the left rear corner, tipping his chair over backward, Jay Cobb drew the Colt's on his right thigh and fanned and fired three times at J. B. Books.

His first round missed its mark. It hit the cash register, slicing the first column of keys from the machine, then ricocheted upward and off the ceiling.

His movement triggered another. Serrano on the instant pulled his Peacemaker from beneath the table, turning in his chair. In the interval between Cobb's first and second rounds, Cross-eye shot the youth through the chest.

Cobb fired a second round at Books while falling across a table, and a third while writhing in agony to the floor.

His second round struck the mirror behind the bar. A split of quicksilver spread from end to end. His third blew three shelves of glassware into a phenomenon of light. A cascade of shards tinkled brilliantly to the floor and bar top.

The effects of low-velocity slugs fired at close range from weapons of heavy caliber, .38s and .45s, are massive. Serrano had sent a bullet through Jay Cobb's rib cage from the right side at a distance of nine feet. After encountering bone, entering the chest cavity anteriorly, the slug tumbled through the lower lobe of the left lung, macerating it, before exiting posteriorly through the rib cage on the left side, tearing an exit wound the size of a fist. With such force was the round driven into and through and out of the body that bits and pieces of bone and shirt were found adhering to the rear-wall mural the following day, together with gobbets of lung tissue, pink and gray in color.

Jay Cobb lay still upon the floor. He was not, however, dead.

The Constantinople was unsuited, acoustically, to gunfire. Not only were the explosions magnified, they were prolonged. They crashed back and forth between the walls, they boomed from tile floor to high ceiling and downward again. They reverberated and echoed and re-echoed within the chamber of the saloon. They made awful demands upon the ears.

There was an intermission.

Books, his back turned, had not moved. Nor had he permitted himself to be surprised that Serrano had elected to shoot at Jay Cobb rather than at him. To be surprised during a gunfight, he had long ago learned, was to be dead.

He drained his glass. After this, he walked along to the street end of the bar, rounded it, stepped over a snow of glassware to the center, found a bottle of white wine, filled his glass, and facing the room from behind the bar, considering Pulford and the man in the derby hat, who had been surprised, and Serrano as they eyed each other and him, sipped wine again.

When the echoes in the room had faded, the aftermath of silence was broken by a sucking sound.

Jay Cobb had incurred what doctors call a "sucking wound." He had hauled himself to hands and knees, and since one lung had collapsed, the macerated left, as he breathed laboriously by means of the right lung, air was drawn loudly through the gaping aperture in his left rib cage.

Now he commenced to crawl from his table toward the bar and, reaching that, toward the front door of the saloon. His progress was slow. His left lung was hemorrhaging, his chest cavity filled with blood. As he attempted to inhale through his mouth, he gagged on blood, and stopped crawling, and coughed a bloody froth. The four men watched him crawl and gag and cough. It was obvious his wound was mortal.

Deliberately therefore, Books drank the last of his wine, put down the glass, drew the Remington from his left-side holster, leaned over the bar, aimed the pistol, and shot Jay Cobb through the head.

He died instantly. The bullet was fired from above and from the rear, an oblique trajectory, at a range of seven feet. It penetrated the temporal bone above and forward of the ear, exposing the brain, passed through the brain, carrying with it segments of skull, and exited through the right orbit, or eye socket, taking off the ethmoid plate and the bridge of the nose. On the tile floor under what remained of Jay Cobb's face lay an eyeball and the brain matter which housed the accumulated knowledge of his twenty years, a grayish, adhesive slop of girls and kings and arithmetic and cows and prayer and mountains but primarily of how to fire a revolver accurately and hate himself and deliver milk and cream and butter.

But while Books's attention was concentrated on this work of mercy, Jack Pulford took advantage of the opportunity.

Standing at his table in the front, he slipped the Smith & Wesson rapidly from his hip and shot the ugly man in the left shoulder.

Books reeled backward, steadied himself with a left hand behind him on a shelf. His pistol was already leveled over the bar, at the fallen Cobb. It turned on his wrist and fired. The bullet struck Jack Pulford in the heart.

He was staggered by the impact, driven against the wall, and slumping down it, continued to fire randomly at Books, emptying the Smith & Wesson into the bar instead. This firing was reflexive, an act of tendon spasm rather than conceived assault. The gambler was dead before he attained a seated position, back to the wall. Books had fired from sixteen feet. His round had entered Jack Pulford's white silk shirt near a diamond stud slightly to the left of the sternum, or breastplate, and torn through the antrioventricular groove. The heart was literally cleaved in two. Yet there was no exit wound in his back, for the heart muscle, tough and fibrous, poses a real impediment, even to a bullet.

Simultaneously, as Pulford and Books began their exchange, Serrano took his Peacemaker from the table, stood, and fired five rounds in Books's general direction. Not one was accurate, for Books had been hit in the left shoulder, and his left hand on a shelf would not sustain him. It gave way, and as he sank backward, a moving, diminishing target, he shot four times at Serrano. His slugs chipped plaster, ripped tables, screamed away into corners. Cross-eye's spiderwebbed the mirror behind the bar with cracks and disintegrated that glassware still intact.

One of Books's shots having plowed a furrow cross the table top inches from his elbow, Koopmann plunged under the table at which he and *El Tuerto* had been seated, in this precipitous process knocking the derby hat from his head.

Through a sleet of glass Books disappeared behind the bar.

*        *        *

The door of the telephone booth opened. A man in a brown suit emerged, a salesman evidently, who had been trapped in the booth while calling a prospective customer, for he carried a leather sample case. Looking neither to left nor right, ignoring the combatants, stepping abstractedly over Jay Cobb's body, he tramped through the open doors of the saloon and took an incurious departure.

There was another intermission.

Had the salesman not guided on the daylight from the doors, he might have been unable to find his way out of the Constantinople. So many rounds had been fired, so much black powder burned, that the room was surcharged with smoke. It did not hang inert. The fans made it into veils and wreaths which turned and twisted and lifted and dropped as the blades revolved. In the midst of death, the black smoke was alive.

Jay Cobb lay on the tiles near the street end of the bar. Jack Pulford sat upright against the wall in an attitude of thought. Koopmann hunched on all fours under the protection of a table in the center of the room. Down on one knee beside the table, Serrano reloaded his pistol. J. B. Books sat in broken glass upon the wooden slatting behind the bar, bleeding only moderately. Pulford's soft-lead slug, fired from sixteen feet, had passed completely through his left shoulder, missing fortunately the subclavian artery but cracking the clavicle and tearing the deltoid muscle and the upper margin of the trapezius. His left arm was stunned and useless.

He put down his empty weapon. His back was to the wooden lockers. Leaning against them, by contorting his right forearm and wrist, he drew the other Remington from the right-side holster on his vest and laid it on his lap. He next removed his Stetson and placed it beside him, noting nearby the dollar bill he had put on the bar for his first glass of wine. Looking up, he saw something remarkable. The glass still stood on the bar, undamaged, and now and then, as the black smoke swirled, sunlight through the front doors of the saloon illumined the glass.

He waited. Koopmann he had seen go under a table. Serrano could not know if he, Books, were dead or alive behind the bar, but a man bent on killing would have to find out. Closing his fingers around the pearl handle of the second Remington in his lap, Books watched the wineglass on the bar top and waited.

Within a minute, when sunlight turned the glass translucent, it darkened suddenly, a darkening which passed from right to left. He could hear no footstep, but the movement of the dark meant to him that someone—it had to be Cross-eye—had skulked along the front of the bar toward the street end.

Books raised his left knee and, laying the barrel of the pistol over it, sighted on the edge of the street end of the bar, and waited. He could feel the wound in his shoulder drain, the slow seepage of blood upon his skin. It was like being leeched.

Then, three feet above the floor, around the edge of the bar, an eye appeared, the Mexican's good eye, and Books fired.

His bullet totally smashed Serrano's globe, or eyeball, spattering floor and bar and locker doors with the gelatinous substance of the eyeball. Slivers of bone were driven by the round through the brain, and a triangle of skull and hair was lifted out at the exit wound in the occipital area. Serrano tumbled backward to lie on his side near Jay Cobb.

There was another intermission.

A man strayed through the front doors of the Constantinople to have a drink. Gasping, he peered into the gunpowder haze. He saw a young man lying near him face down in the slime of his own brains, and a Mexican next to him with a gaping hole in his skull, and a third man seated on the floor against the left-hand wall wearing a white silk shirt soaked with blood, and a fourth man, alive, cowering under a table.

"Dear God," said the stray, and backed through the doors.

His were the first words spoken.

Koopmann crawled from under the table, retrieved his derby, and settled it on his head.

"Books!" he shouted.

There was no response from behind the bar.

"I am trowing to you my gun, Books!" His accent was German. "I vant oud of dis, Books, zo I am trowing to you my gun!"

Koopmann sailed his Navy Colt's over the bar.

"Dere!"

On the sly, he reached for, picked up the revolver Jay Cobb had dropped when first hit, and concealed it behind his back.

"I am standing now up, Books, and valking oud of here!"

Koopmann stood, kept the revolver behind his back in his right hand and, turning to keep the weapon out of sight, began to walk ponderously toward the doors.

"I am now going. I am braying to Gott you vill led me, Books."

He was a big man with round, red cheeks, and now, passing along the bar, passing what might be behind it, his eyes began to perspire tears which rolled down his round, red cheeks.

"I am braying to Gott, Books!" he shouted. "Dat you vill led me valk oud of dis place alife!"

Behind the bar, Books came to his knees, shoved the Remington into a coat pocket, extended his right arm to seize hold of the cold water tap over the sink, and pulled himself to his feet. Koopmann had passed Jay Cobb's body and moved the revolver around to his chest and was now near the doors.

Putting his weight against the bar to keep himself erect, Books drew the pistol from his coat pocket, leveled it, and shot Koopmann in the back.

The round was well placed. It entered the torso in the intercostal space between the ribs, missing the spine but mangling the paravertebral muscles, and exited by breaking out a wide swatch of the sternum, or breastbone. Koopmann dropped the Colt's, hugged his chest, and staggered several more steps toward the doors. But the aortic root had been transected, severed by the bullet. The pumping of the heart builds enormous pressure in the human vascular system, which was suddenly released. Blood sprayed from the outlet in his breast as though from the nozzle of a hose, drenching tables and chairs and tiles, so that by the time Koopmann hit the floor he splashed into a pool of his own blood, for he was practically exsanguinated.

*          *          *

It was ended.

The roar of gunfire receded, died. Suspended from the ceiling on their stems, the blades of the four fans rotated, stirring the caldron of black smoke. The sound they made, however, the only sound in the room, was no longer that of breathing, of soft and rhythmic respiration. They sighed. They seemed to sigh an endless, electrical dirge for the repose of the dead below.

Books stood at the bar, weapon in hand, looking down at Koopmann's body.

Behind him the barkeep, Murray, stepped through the archway from the gambling room, sized the situation, put a double-barreled 10-gauge Parker shotgun to his shoulder, aimed, and fired one barrel, then the other, into Books's back.

The shootist was blown away from the bar, blown over, blown down, falling into the walkway between bar and lockers.

Shotgun shells were loaded with a heavy powder charge. And in this case they contained No. 4 bird shot, which spread into a pattern the diameter of a plate and were intended to maim a man, even at close range, rather than to kill. They penetrated Books's coat, vest, shirt, underwear, and skin, they lacerated much muscle, a few pellets entered the chest cavity, and there was some external bleeding, but the wounds were scarcely fatal.

Knowing this, the barkeep stepped immediately back through the archway into the gambling room again, out of sight, to reload.

Books lay on his belly. Drawing up his legs, he pushed with his feet against the bar and switched

himself so that he lay prone again, facing the opposite direction, facing the archway. There was
still no feeling in his left arm. With his right he
pulled at the left, bending it at the elbow, placing
the forearm before him, and settling his chin upon
the wrist. Then, clawing in broken glass with his
good hand, he located the Remington he had just
fired and, extending his right arm on the slatting,
pointed the revolver at the archway.

He was not surprised that he had been shot
from the rear, but he did not know who had done
it. He had killed the men he wanted to. But someone was still trying to kill him, and even in a state
of total shock, instinct required him to defend
himself.

Gun in hand, bleeding moderately from the
wounds in his left shoulder and back, he waited.

In a minute or two Murray poked his head around
the molding of the archway to have a look.

Books fired, and missed.

Astonished that the gun man still had fight in
him, the barkeep ducked away again, out of sight.

He thought: All of them needed killing, and it is
done. I have hurt like this before. That one in the
gut, over in Bisbee. I have hurt worse than that,
though, but till now I disremembered it. Once,
when we were kids, the four of us, we got into
some real mischief. It was over in San Saba County.
One day my mother hooked a yoke of oxen up to a
wagon and went to a neighbor's and told us to be
good and left us alone, Em and Clara, my sisters,
and my little brother Joe and me. I have not seen
them since I was sixteen. I wish I knew what has

become of them, if they are well and happy, for they were dear to me. God bless them. Well, no sooner was she gone than we went to it. There was a barrel of homemade molasses in the kitchen, but no bread, so we got a caddy of tobacco from under my pa's bed. A caddy held twenty-five plugs, as I recollect. We would take a plug of tobacco and dip it in the molasses and then lick the molasses off the tobacco. After enough licks, we took powerfully sick. We had bellyaches as big as Texas. How we howled and carried on till Ma came home. We thought we were about to die and would just as soon. So I have hurt like this before. I have not seen them since I was sixteen. God bless them.

Gillom Rogers inched through the doors of the Constantinople. Eyes watering from the smoke, he gaped at Jay Cobb and Serrano and Koopmann, and at Jack Pulford, seated against the wall.

Skirting the three bodies near the bar, avoiding the blood and brains as best he could, he looked over the bar, then scuffed in wonder through the carnage of glass behind it. A dollar bill stopped him. He put it in the pants pocket which held the other money. A black-handled Remington lay in the walkway. He picked it up and holding his breath approached the prone man, who seemed small to him now, even puny.

"Mister Books?"

He saw the torn coat and the blood on it and the right arm extended stiffly, gun aimed. He moved slowly to Books's side, bending.

"It's me, Gillom," he said.

He got down on his knees. Books was incapable of speech. His chin was clamped upon his left wrist.

Gillom did not care to look into the face, but the eyes arrested him. They considered. They considered not only the archway, as though something implacable waited on the other side, but something transcendent beyond that as well, far beyond.

"Mister Books, it's me, Gillom."

The mouth opened. Nothing audible issued from it, but the lips formed two words: "kill" and "me."

"Kill you?"

Gillom chewed his lips.

"Sure thing," he said, then stood, moved behind the man, straddled him, and put the muzzle of the revolver he had picked up to the back of the head. He turned his own head away; shut his eyes tight; gritted his teeth; pulled the trigger.

The hammer clicked.

"Shit," he groaned.

He despaired, aware on the rim of his consciousness of the smoke and the reek of the air and the solemnity of the fans. He got down on his knees again beside the prone man and worked at the fingers clenching the pearl handle of the second Remington, prying them free until he possessed that weapon too.

He stood again, straddled the prone man, and put the muzzle of the revolver to the back of John Bernard Books's head a second time, into the hair. He turned his own head away; shut his eyes tight; gritted his teeth; and pulled the trigger.

He walked out of the Constantinople into chaste air. A crowd of men and boys had gathered across the street. Waiting for a buggy to pass, then a buckboard, he crossed the street to the crowd.

"What happened in there?"

At least six asked.

"They're all dead," said Gillom.

"Who?"

"J. B. Books. Jay Cobb. Jack Pulford. A Mex name of Serrano, a rustler. And some guy I don't know who. A big guy. He killed 'em all."

"Who?"

"Books."

Someone had counted. "Five! Whooeee!"

"Jesus Christ, boys, he killed every hard case around!" someone exulted. "Jesus, boys, we fin'ly got us a clean town!"

"Oughta put up a statue of the murderin' bastard!" someone enthused.

"These are his guns." Gillom held them up for all to covet. "He gave 'em to me before he died."

"Look at that!"

"Short barrel, no sight, specials by God—hey, kid, want to sell 'em?"

"Hell, no," said Gillom. He grinned and waved at the Constantinople. "O. K., folks, step right over and see the show! Drinks on the house!"

As the crowd strided across the street, Gillom Rogers strode away down it, swinging a gun in each hand. An alchemy of false spring sunlight turned the nickel of the Remingtons to silver. He strode head up, shoulders back, taller to himself, having sensations he had never known before. One gun was still warm in his hand, the bite of smoke was in his nose and the taste of death on his tongue. His heart was high in his gullet, the danger past—and now the sweat, suddenly, and the nothingness, and the sweet clean feel of being born.